THE
Fargus
Technique

THE
Fargus
Technique

David Mangum

THOMAS Y. CROWELL COMPANY
New York · Established 1834

Designed by Jill Schwartz

MANUFACTURED IN THE UNITED STATES OF AMERICA

ISBN 0-690-28964-2

1 2 3 4 5 6 7 8 9 10

Library of Congress Cataloging in Publication Data

Mangum, David.
  The Fargus technique.
  I. Title.
PZ4.M2756Far   [PS3563.A48]   813'.5'4   73-1897

For Mr. Hull, Mrs. Donley, and Denson

But the worst enemy you can encounter will always be you, yourself; you lie in wait for yourself in caves and woods.

Lonely one, you are going the way to yourself.

—NIETZSCHE, Thus Spoke Zarathustra

Part I

The Fisherman's Marina clings like a cluster of forgotten ticks to the last slowly sloping bank before the log road out of Ridgeland runs into the lake. Walls that once were billboards before being surreptitiously transplanted by the proprietress and her henchmen, the water rats, thud gently to the bass of the country jukebox and the tilt of the pinball machine; studded with the stapled envelopes of fishhooks, sinkers, and bright bobbers, they tap time to the music, the wind, or their own encroaching collapse. In the shed out back, the bait crickets sing and creep in their cages to the accompaniment of the gurgling aerators in the minnow vats for an audience of cantankerous outboards, perched on sawhorses like fantastic birds, and for the king snake that lives beneath the floor. Moored to the sagging, malodorous pier a rod farther in the lake, the tar-caulked cypress skiffs sink a little lower every year until the oldest among them is completely water-logged and awash.

After the morning rush of serious fishermen, the proprietress guards her King Edward cashbox from a stool, and her husband, Charlie, chief water rat, crawls out from wherever he collapsed the night before to begin plotting some means of getting around his wife and into the cooler for the day's first beer. The woman is vicious and industrious; she runs the marina; whereas Charlie's forte is craft, refusing heavy work on the grounds of his war wound, light work because it belongs to the woman, and taking credit for all because the lease of the lakeshore lot from the Jackson man who owns it is in his name. Charlie's face in the front door brings a barrage of vulgar abuse from the woman, but if her tongue is incisive, her gums are toothless: Charlie invariably gets his beer; and she receives a malfragrant kiss of thanks above the left eye.

This is the time when Charlie comes into his own. The day as good as wasted already, every bummer and water rat along the lakeshore comes limping out of the woods, or driving an overheating, oil-burning pickup, to sit on the pier with Charlie, drinking beer and spitting tobacco juice at the baby sunfish that swarm among the pilings. Charlie is considered something of an authority on the subjects of sex, alcohol, and niggers—the water rats' major topics of interest. He has had intercourse with humans of four races and two sexes, and with several species of animals, and by virtue of his bootlegging activities before the state went wet, he knows which brands of beer have the most alcohol and which moonshines are safely free of lead. Niggers are fair game for all, Charlie being needed only to settle disputes.

The South must have a thousand places like this.

Nothing ever really disturbs a place like The Fisherman's Marina. They are found at the ends of dirt roads that few even know exist. So when Charlie and his friends saw a rich man get out of a taxi and go into the bar one blustery March morning, they hardly turned their heads. And a half hour later when a floatplane landed in the lake, and the rich man came out and climbed aboard, and the plane took off, they didn't think much of that either. When rich men's concerns went smoothly, it rarely concerned Charlie and his friends.

And they certainly didn't realize that the big, clean-looking, curly-headed rich man flying the airplane was a nigger.

1

Henry Fargus, a gynecologist from Jackson, was discernible as a rich man only because of his expensive fishing rod and Mitchell reel. He was dressed, like Charlie, in khaki pants and a plaid wool shirt, carrying his packs to a table and setting them down like an old man at the end of a long and rocky road. For a moment his back remained stooped; then he sat down, and the woman came and took his order for a beer.

The jukebox was playing "Does My Ring Hurt Your Finger When You Go Out at Night?" Fargus idly tapped his fingers.

He was a short man, rather heavy without being fat. His face was scarcely wrinkled for a man well past forty. It was clean and shaven, and the thick gun-metal hair was freshly combed, but there was in Fargus' eyes and cheeks a knowledge or a worry which only his humorous mouth kept from making him look old. He looked up and smiled when the woman brought his beer. She scribbled something on a pad and put the ticket on a wet spot in front of him. Fargus frowned at this; the water was soaking through and turning the back of the ticket brown. But the woman was gone. Fargus shrugged, pursed his humorous mouth, and resumed tapping the table, staring idly at the beer can.

A while later, when the plane landed, he paid his soaked bill and resumed his load, leaving the beer untouched.

Arnold Weathermore was standing at the end of the pier, holding his Cessna by a wing strut when Fargus came out. He was a big man, lithe and powerfully built, with a high crop of curly—though not kinky—black hair. His face was strikingly handsome with high cheekbones, a massive brow, and full sensuous lips. He stood on the rotten boards in an attitude of poised, suspended power, darting his black eyes nervously from Fargus to the cowed water rats, and resentfully back to Fargus. On a leather thong around his neck a sterling silver peace symbol twirled in the freshening wind. Weathermore was a psychiatrist making his present home in St. Louis.

When Fargus came within reach of his free hand, Weathermore snatched the pack and tossed it like nothing into the plane's back seat. "Let's get out of this hole," he said to Fargus, but loud enough for everyone to hear, "I don't like the looks of those bastards sitting on the porch."

Fargus winced, glancing back toward Charlie, and when he turned back around, Arnold was looking at his own reflection in the airplane window, patting his hair into shape—into what Fargus suddenly realized was the wind-wrecked remains of a hand-teased afro. Fargus shook his head and monkey-climbed after his friend into the cabin.

Arnold spun the prop, and raindrops, like a hail of bullets, raked across the windshield. Arnold gentled his pontoons away from the pier, then swung into the wind and shoved the throttle wide. Fargus watched the sheet of spray change as the pontoons planed off. Weathermore was serious about his flying: he never talked during a takeoff or a landing. Fargus watched the spray do crazy things with the shore-line shapes. The upholstery pushed around his buttocks with the power of the plane, rocking him backward as it lifted from the surface, leaving him one last instant's clear view of civilized shoreline. Weathermore swept the airplane wide and into the south, and although Fargus could see nothing now except gray sky, the picture of the shoreline stayed with him. He watched Arnold relax.

"Weather looks great," Fargus remarked.

"Couldn't be better," Weathermore said with serious sarcasm, switching on the windshield wipers. "In fact, if it gets much better I'm scared the fish are gonna be suspicious."

"These fish, Arnold—" Fargus gestured with his hands, indicating the length of a true lunker—"these fish! Why I may be scared to step in the water. They may bite us!"

"I know your fish stories."

"You wait," pouted Fargus.

"Spotted weakfish," said Weathermore derogatorily, using the northern expression.

"Speckled trout! And ten-pound reds to pop the guides off those fairy-wand fly rods of yours. Arnold, unless you had the foresight to bring a surf rod, you're not gonna have a chance."

"I beg your pardon, white man. I have had my rodmaker build me a ten-foot surf rod which I'm going to give you at the end of this ill-conceived 'vacation' of ours. There's not but one thing that could make me stoop to fishing for spotted weakfish."

4

"And what's that?"

"Don't make me say it, Hank."

"All right, then, don't say it."

"Pity, Fargus! Pity!"

"Well, never mind."

"No. I don't care about myself. There I was. Up there in the big city making it, you know? But when you asked me, I thought there's ole Fargus down there in Jackson, Mississippi. Not making it, you know? Been working his tail off for two years trying to rid the world of twat rot. And he wants a vacation. What else could I do?"

"That's right, what else?"

"I mean, I owe something to friendship, to old time's sake." Weathermore fingered his peace symbol.

"Oh, is that what I am?"

"That's what your whole goddam state is. I may be the only black man in the world who has a soft spot in his heart for a Mississippian."

"You may be the only nigger in the States who has to tease his hair to get it into an afro. Are you sure you wouldn't be better off with Dixie Peach Pomade?"

"After the revolution there won't be any more Dixie Peach Pomade. No Mississippi either, for that matter."

"Well tell me this," Fargus said. "How do you convince all these people that you're a nigger? I mean that flop on your head doesn't fool anybody."

"Soul, Fargus! I've got soul!"

"I guess you've quit calling yourself a psychiatrist and started calling yourself a soul doctor."

"I may do that, Fargus; I just may." Weathermore extracted a pipe from his jacket pocket, the bowl of which was carved in the image of his own head. It was a meerschaum, in the process of turning from white to brown.

Jackson, Fargus' town, was disappearing behind them. Fargus turned and watched it go. He watched it shrink away from him as the airplane banked into heavier clouds in the direction of the river.

"Lord have mercy on such as we," Fargus said. "Arnold, do you mind if I ask you when you started telling people about this?"

5

"Well—it was last August."

"And the occasion?"

Arnold glared. "What's it to you, man?"

"Well, ever since your old man's funeral I've been thinking I was the only person in the land of the living who knew your—ah—dark secret."

"Hades," Arnold spat. Then he softened. "Aw, I know it. But there's something you didn't know. A lot."

"Such as?"

"Oh—feelings I've had. Ever since the movement began."

"What movement?"

"The civil rights movement, man!"

"Hell, Arnold, what feelings?"

"Well, have you ever watched a flock of white geese in the fall when the wild ones start flying over?"

"Can't say I have."

"They get restless, Hank. No matter how many generations away from the wild they are, no matter how much they've been tamed and caged and had their behavior modified and their color changed to suit the needs of somebody besides themselves, when they hear that wild call, they get the urge to break out and be free to be their wild selves."

"And so," Fargus said, "when you saw a bunch of crazy niggras getting squirted with firehoses, your wild self just demanded that you jump in and get squirted, too."

"It was merely an attempt to help you understand," Weathermore said.

"Well, I'm glad to hear that," Fargus said. "I was beginning to think you were trying to tell me you were part goose, too."

"Very funny, Fargus."

"So inside one month you changed your race and went from an Ole Miss M.D. to a bona fide freedom rider."

"It isn't that simple. My whole life is involved."

"Arnold, you're unbelievable," said Fargus.

Weathermore turned and looked at him. Fargus was serious.

"Tell me this," Fargus said. "Now that you're in a position to know. Is it true what Faulkner said: If you've ever been a nigger on a Saturday night, you'll never want to be white again?"

"He had no conception of what it's like to be a black man in America today," Weathermore said.

Fargus said nothing. He was looking out the window again.

Weathermore adjusted his throttle. The sky was darkening in the south. Weathermore wondered if Fargus was noticing the way he kept compensating for the heavy gusts with a slight touch of rudder.

Fargus was amazed at himself for the way he kept catching himself looking back toward Jackson. There was nothing out the window but sky and greenish-gray earth, but he kept feeling the city behind him. "What happened to us, Arnold?" he said, staring at Weathermore's afro. The words were out before he knew it, so he was amazed again.

"I don't know about you," Weathermore said, tossing his head and glancing quickly at Fargus, "but what's happened to me is, I'm a free man."

"Right on," said Fargus, making a fist and looking out the window again. He suddenly didn't want to think about what was happening to them. He wanted to think about the fishing. He wanted to think about the sand and the wind and cold water. Free men—I didn't come on this trip to think about that. He was staring hard at a gray line on the horizon far to the northeast.

"What the hell's eating you?" Weathermore asked.

Fargus turned around and looked at him. "Nothing's eating me."

A heavy gust rocked the plane. "Shit," said Weathermore, hitting the rudder but too late. Then he stared at Fargus, thinking. "Say, man, what you runnin' from?"

"What do you care?" Fargus cracked.

"What do you mean, What do I care? It's not every white man that I'd just drop everything for and take off into the black heart of Mississippi with, just because he has to go fishing three months too early to catch anything besides spotted weakfish."

"Look, do you think you could just forget that white man stuff?"

"Lord, you are in a bad mood, aren't you?"

"Well, I didn't exactly call you up because I was enjoying myself."

"Well, what is it? Is your research bothering you?"

Fargus said nothing.

"Your wife?"

"No!"

"Well, excuse me."

"Well, she does have a name, Arnold."

"Little Miss Magnolia Blossom—Aw, come on, Hank. This is me—Arnold!"

"Aw, I know. I'm sorry. I just don't even want to talk about it. I don't even want to think about it. The reason I wanted to go fishing was because I wanted to get away from thinking about it."

"Okay. Well, just take it easy, then, okay? Just relax and don't think about it, and it'll be all right."

"Thanks, buddy," Fargus said. He turned to Weathermore and managed a weak smile.

And Fargus didn't want to think about it. Which is why he couldn't think of anything else.

Because if I think about it, I'll start thinking about that dog, Fargus thought, and that's just what I don't want to do. Because the dog's dead. Dead in the fall, two years ago. A two-year winter.

For the first time all day the humor vanished from Fargus' mouth. He stretched his tired neck and gazed out into the hazy air, and when Arnold seemed unable to think of anything else to say, he relented.

Sunday, the first one that fall when the cold stuck clear through to afternoon. The house quiet like always since Freddy and Cindy married. Alice was knitting. A football game was on the TV, but the sound was off. I was turning the pages of the thick Sunday paper—not reading, just turning, my thoughts as pointless and incessant as the working of Alice's needles.

Then, out of the corner of my eye, I saw the collie, the last of the kids' pets, struggling across the lawn. I could tell she was in pain, ought to be put out of her misery; but Alice's nerves are delicate these days. The old dog walked around herself three times before she lay down in the sun. I turned a page.

A man had won a prize for growing a hundred and twenty pound watermelon . . . a steamboat being lifted from the Yazoo River. Alice was humming a lullaby, knitting for Cindy's kid. Then I glanced out the window again.

The dog hadn't moved. Except it seemed like one leg was

sticking up in the air. I folded the paper and went to the door. Alice smiled at me on the way out. Her eyes were wet. I smiled back.

I walked across the lawn and over to the dog. Then I glanced back up at the window. Alice hadn't seen. So I picked up the dog and carried it around back and up the little hill in the corner of the yard to take its place among the cats and turtles and goldfish that had preceded it into the ground.

The afternoon growing colder. I had to hurry with the shovel. Colder than I'd thought. So cold I caught a stitch in my side and something like a giggle escaped. Then, patting the final shovelful into place, I thought of something to giggle at: "Henry Fargus, Pussyplumber—1925–1968." I thought about going back down to the house and telling Alice, her not saying much the rest of the night. Alluvasudden, I thought I couldn't stand it.

The next morning I was in the office of Clemens, senior partner of Clemens, Baskins, Fargus, and Bunch—Ob. Gyn. Clemens is a small, bearded man, too old to see patients. He only keeps his office for consultations. And because he has nowhere else to go.

"Dr. Clemens," I said, "I gotta get out of here for a while and get something off my mind."

"Oh? Like what?"

"I'm not exactly sure."

"Well, what do you want me to do about it?"

"I want a grant—from the clinic. And an indefinite sabbatical."

"A grant for what?"

"Some research."

"Indeed? Well, Henry, you know the only grant you could get from this clinic would be something like nine hundred a month—"

"I'll take it!"

Clemens blinked. The old lab coat he wore was permanently stained. "Do you mind," he said, "if I ask why you want to give up your practice for nine hundred a month?"

"I don't know. Something scared me real bad yesterday. And I'm not sure why."

"I see," he said. "And is the research you have in mind gynecological in nature?"

"Yes. I think I want to do something in the area of yeast infections."

9

"Yeast? Something must have scared you. Why yeast?"

Then I exploded: "What do you mean, Why yeast? Do you have any idea what I do every day? I look up thirty pussies a day, and twenty of them will be full of yeast! White people. Niggras. Blond pussies. Brunette pussies. Everybody's got yeast, Clemens. And there's not a damned thing I can do about it. 'Mrs. Jones, you've got a yeast infection.' 'You're telling me! I've had a yeast infection for thirty years!' 'Mrs. Lee, you've got a yeast infection. Nothing to be alarmed at, but very pesky.' 'Oh, no!—venereal dizzeze!' I've got a yeast infection on my soul, Clemens, and I'm getting too old for that!"

Clemens tapped his pipestem and sadly shook his head. On his desk was a ceramic model of the female urogenital system given me once by an unmarried and unmoneyed sculptress for whom I delivered a baby. Clemens had liked it, so I gave it to him. He pushed it toward me and blinked. "It is a dangerous situation," he said, "and a dangerous object for desperation."

But he gave me the grant.

By the time the first freeze hit, I was out of Clemens, Baskins, Fargus, and Bunch, Ob. Gyn., and into a tiny cubicle off the cytology lab in the Ole Miss Medical Center, working on the Fargus pH control technique for vaginal yeast infections. And every night before I went to bed, I was reading a biography of Jonas Salk.

"Weathermore," Fargus said, "Do you have any idea what it's like to work on anything as hard as I worked on that Fargus technique?"

"Why," said Weathermore skeptically, "I guess not."

"It's hell," said Fargus. "I mean, everybody you see, you want to go up to them and talk about it because it's just the only thing in the world you've got on your mind. And they just look at you like you're nuts."

"Yeah?"

"I mean, it's very beautiful, if I can just solve a couple of problems. You know yeast can't grow in an acid environment—"

Sensing an advantage, Weathermore scowled.

"I guess you don't want to hear about it either, then."

Weathermore was momentarily puzzled. "What about Alice?" he said tentatively. "What did she think about all this?"

"She didn't say much," Fargus said. She never said much about anything these days. But Fargus didn't want to think about Alice. He wanted to think about the fishing.

"Henry," Alice had said, "I don't understand it at all."

"Alice, the kids are gone," he had answered. "The house is paid off. I promise, you won't suffer for a thing."

"Well, I just don't want to talk about it."

"It's really very beautiful—"

"I don't want to hear it."

"She avoids crises," Fargus said to Arnold.

"What?"

"This time of life; she avoids crises."

"I bet," said Weathermore. "Thank God, that's one crisis I've managed to avoid. I think now that I've made it this far, I won't have to worry about it anymore."

"Right," said Fargus. He knew of two proposals Weathermore had made. Both times the courtships had been brief and stormy, with loud protestations of love on Weathermore's part. Both times they had ended abruptly. Weathermore had claimed, "We just decided it wouldn't work"; but Fargus believed he had been turned down. Those were the only times Fargus knew of when Weathermore had had anything to do with women. "Just lay off Alice, okay?" he said.

"I wouldn't say a word, Hank," Weathermore grinned. "Well, tell me this then, What did happen?"

"Well, nothing has really happened yet."

"But the Fargus technique isn't coming along too well?"

"I didn't say that. Fargus isn't coming along too well. I really don't want to talk about this, Arnold; honest—"

"Okay. Okay. Scuse me." Weathermore stared at the windshield. Fargus stared out the window.

The weather was worsening; the flying was rough.

"Do you know," Fargus said, "what I did that winter when I was really going on it?"

11

"What's that?"

"I was up in that little ole box of a room putting in like eighteen hours a day over a microscope, and my neck would get to cramping and my eyes burning, and one day when it really started getting bad, I got a three-by-five note card and cut it in the shape of a headstone and wrote 'Henry Fargus, Pussyplumber' on it."

Weathermore grinned.

"It helped!"

2

In the sky through which Fargus and Weathermore were flying, the spring equinox was making weather. It was late March. To the north of them, the North American landmass was cold; and to the south, the Gulf of Mexico was warm and damp with the coming of spring. Ahead of the Cessna, the two fronts were skirmishing like armies with brief, wicked flare-ups of lightning and scattered turbulences of rain and wind that made flying rough.

Weathermore knew he was a good pilot. Now he was getting to use it. He wondered if Fargus could tell the way he more or less flew "by the seat of his pants," the way his nerves went out into the wings and sensed the air currents, so that every variation brought about an instantaneous response through the controls. He imagined Fargus watching him and thinking about the difference between him and other pilots. Because they had to think that about him. No matter what anybody might think about him, they had to know he was a good pilot.

He glanced across at Fargus. Fargus was looking out the window.

"Why didn't you ever take out a private pilot's license?" Weathermore said hopefully.

Fargus shrugged.

"You were a pilot then."

"Just a B-17," said Fargus.

"You could get one easy."

"I just don't want to be a pilot anymore."

Weathermore shrugged. Then suddenly he turned on Fargus and shot back, "Why the hell not?"

"I just don't want to," Fargus said absently without turning from the window.

Well, screw you then. You presume one helluva lot on a person, don't you, Fargus? Call a guy up and get him to cancel everything he's got planned to take you fishing. And what the hell? I did it.

"Hank baby!" Weathermore had said when he heard Fargus' voice. "How are things in the jungle?"

"Steamy and hot, you bastard. We're going fishing." Just like that!

"You crazy, man? There ain't a drop of running water north of the border."

"That's right," Fargus said. "We're going south."

"South where?"

"South of Mississippi! Chandeleur Islands for specks and redfish."

"Aw, Hank, you must be schitz. You know I don't go for specks and reds."

"You're going," Fargus said flatly.

"Lissen, I really would like to, but I got all kinds of meetings and appointments—"

"So break 'em."

"I mean with important people," Weathermore pled.

"Whom?"

"NAACP."

"Yeah. Well, I already canceled the attack on Peking I was planning," Fargus said.

"No, man, I mean it. Didn't I tell you? I'm a free man. I'm telling the world. I'm black and I'm proud."

"Just as long as you keep shut up about it down here," Fargus said, "or I'll have the Klan on you."

"Seriously, man—"

"Be here," Fargus said flatly.

Good old Hank! "Say, Hank, are you on the lam? What is it? The Fargus technique causes painful and irregular b.m.'s?"

"Only in its father," Fargus said, "and transvestitism in his soul brother if that plane isn't here at four Thursday."

"Okay, man," Weathermore had said, "I'll see what I can do—"
And the son-of-a-bitching Fargus had hung up.
*And Weathermore had been there, four o'clock Thursday. Although
now he could not figure out why.*

"Mississippi," sneered Weathermore as they flew momentarily
out of a cloud and the state was spread below them, "the most lied-
about state in the nation. Get your valentine in Dixie or get your
donkey out." He tried to laugh.

"Say it loud, huh?" Fargus said.

"I'm black and I'm proud," said Weathermore defensively.

"Hey," said Fargus. "What's that thing around your neck?"

"Peace symbol?" He raised his brows.

"Yeah? Where I come from that's the sign of the anti-Christ."

"I hope it works out that way," Weathermore said.

"Whew," said Fargus, turning suddenly now to face him. "You
are black and proud, aren't you?"

"I wish the anti-Christ would eat this whole damn state."

Fargus laughed. "Aw, now," he said, "just cause you can't recon-
cile your new-found niggerness with a degree from Ole Miss is no
reason to start cutting down our home state."

"Mississippi is not my home state!" Weathermore snapped. "I
was raised in New Orleans."

"You were born here," Fargus mocked. "You got all your med
school here." Fargus' eyes were twinkling.

"Screw it," said Weathermore, but he grinned, too. He'd rather
Fargus kidded than ignored him.

"Just think though," said Fargus, "if you hadn't of come to Ole
Miss, we'd never have met."

"Yeah," said Weathermore, relaxing again. It was true.

*They had been on the same dorm floor their freshman year, but they
didn't really meet until one Friday night when most of the floor was at
a dance. Weathermore and all the rest of the hardtails were in one
room having a bull session. All the hardtails except Fargus, that is.
Fargus, Weathermore knew, was in the next room studying. Weathermore had gotten out a fifth of rum from his trunk and was mixing
drinks for everybody. He had always known he was different from the*

14

rest of them, but tonight it was working out that he was being their leader. Most of these rednecks had never tasted rum, much less known how to mix it. They were all homesick, too, so he was talking and they were listening. They were country rednecks, but he knew his way around New Orleans. He was telling them about New Orleans and mixing New Orleans drinks for them.

"What about motherfucker next door?" Arnold said to Billy Green, handing him the last drink.

"Fargus?" Billy Green said.

"What's wrong with him?" Arnold sneered.

"Lay off him," Billy Green said. "His mother just died."

All of a sudden, Weathermore didn't feel good anymore. Here he'd called Fargus a motherfucker, and Fargus' mother had just died. The walls were thin, too, so Fargus had probably heard him. And what was worse, Fargus was Billy Green's friend, and Billy Green knew Fargus had probably heard him. While the rest of the guys drank, Weathermore turned the conversation to religion, how he didn't believe that the ordinary Christianity that the churches peddled was intellectually respectable.

He talked louder and faster.

But he kept picturing Fargus, homesick and depressed in the other room, missing his mother. He suddenly wished he were homesick and missing his mother. He had never been either, and they seemed to him noble afflictions. Why don't you shoot yourself, Weathermore?

Then there was a knock at the door. It couldn't be—the door opened, and it was—Fargus. The words died in Weathermore's throat.

"Hey, you guys," Fargus said. "You reckon you could move down to somebody else's room. I'm trying to study."

Weathermore looked frantically about at the others. The stupid-ass rednecks were ready to go. He had a sudden urge to kill Fargus: that seemed the only way. But Billy Green said, "Aw, come on in and sit down and have a drink. Nobody studies on a Friday night."

None of them wanted to be nobody to Billy Green. Fargus hesitated. Weathermore said nothing. Fargus looked contemptuously at the rum bottle.

"What the heck," Fargus said. "I got some whiskey and branch water stashed in my trunk."

So all the stupid-ass rednecks got up and went over to Fargus' room.

15

Weathermore shrugged, got up, went with them, and shrugged one more time when he got inside the door. "Corn whiskey," he said, "is not bad booze. It's just that most people don't know how to drink it. They think you have to be a hillbilly and drink the stuff straight. Rot! Of course, they don't like it. It's just that most corn is of indeterminate proof and you have to judge with your tongue to know how to mix it properly." Weathermore seized the two bottles and mixed drinks all around, judging the proportions by sticking his finger into the bottle and touching his tongue.

He began talking about the Baptists again, but out of the corner of his eye he saw Fargus toss his drink off fast and reach to mix himself another. "The whole thing is a matter of an individual's intelligence," Weathermore said. He watched Fargus pour himself about four fingers and then add about one of water. No, Weathermore thought, he's not gonna drink that. That's gonna take the top of his young head off. "No reasonably sophisticated person. . . ." Fargus put the glass to his mouth, and Weathermore could see his eyes bug out above the rim. ". . . pure and unadulterated bunkum!" Fargus slammed the glass down on the table. His eyes were very wet.

"Jest wait a minnit," one of the drunkest of the stupid-ass rednecks broke in. "Lemme ast you sump'm I know sump'm about."

"Well—certainly." Weathermore turned to him.

"D'you agree with what my preacher said, That these here new translations of the Bible was inspired by Satan?"

"Of course, I don't," Weathermore said. "The King James Version is completely obsolete." He reached up into Fargus' bookcase and brought down Fargus' Bible. "Screw this translation," he said.

Fargus hit Weathermore first in the eye and then in the mouth. Then, with both fists sounding as they hit Fargus' breastbone like a bale of cotton hitting a steamboat deck, Weathermore sent Fargus sprawling across the desk. Fargus scrambled for the corner and came up with a Louisville slugger baseball bat. Fargus swung the bat like it wasn't his first time and caught Weathermore in the kidneys. Weathermore went down, but before Fargus could recover from the swing, he was back up, shooting a right to Fargus' eye, and Fargus fell at Weathermore's feet with his mouth wide.

Weathermore was sick even as he unballed his fist, and it wasn't his ribs. It was the same old feeling in his stomach, the same old, cold

16

empty feeling that he had thought just tonight he maybe wasn't ever going to have again. Just tonight with all the guys around in his room he had thought that maybe he was never going to have that feeling again, and now all the guys were laughing. How could they enjoy a fight like that? Why in the hell were they laughing at him? All of them except Billy Green.

Billy Green was looking from Fargus to him and back. "Hey, you bastards," Billy Green said, "we got to get him to the infirmary. His head hit that floor pretty hard." One of the rednecks punched another one in the shoulder. They were all laughing. "You better come too for those ribs," he said to Weathermore. Weathermore looked at the rednecks, then reached down and picked up Fargus' feet. Billy Green looked puzzled but then shrugged, and they carried Fargus out the dorm and over to the infirmary. Billy made them both check in and then left, looking disgusted.

They put Fargus and Weathermore in the same empty ward to wait for the X-ray man to come. Fargus was still laid out, but as soon as the nurse left, Weathermore sat up on the bed. His chest was sore, but that wasn't where he hurt worst. He looked at Fargus, the little bastard, and he felt the way he had one time when he saw a birthday party in somebody else's yard when he was a little kid in New Orleans, and he had just gone up and started playing with the rest of the kids; and then one of the mothers had whispered something to one of the other mothers, and they had made him leave. Hell, that was the way he felt most of the time if he was honest.

When Fargus began to move, the cold feeling in Weathermore's stomach became a knot. "Hey, Fargus," he whispered. "You okay?"

"Lord," Fargus said out loud. "You have got a fist."

"Jeezums, man, I'm sorry. But you was—"

"Forget it," Fargus said. "I started it."

"But, I mean, I was just sitting there talking and all of a sudden—"

"Forget it," Fargus said. "I know I started it. You have just got some fist. That's all."

"Oh, Jeezums, man, I'm so sorry."

"Would you quit saying Jeezums." Fargus seemed to Weathermore to be in pain.

"Oh, sure, sure, man," Weathermore said. "But what happened? What was it?"

17

"You said screw that Bible," Fargus said. *"My mother gave me that Bible, and she's dead."*

"Oh, listen, Fargus, I'm sorry. I'm so sorry."

"Forget it," Fargus said. *"I hit you first."*

Weathermore said nothing.

"What are we doing in here?" Fargus said.

"X rays," Weathermore said. *"Your head, my ribs. You don't swing a bad bat yourself."*

"I guess it's my turn to be sorry."

"Forget it. You ever play ball?"

"Second base."

"You know, we're a fine pair of brawlers," Weathermore said. *"Thing lasts ten seconds, and we're both in the hospital."*

"Yeah."

"God," Weathermore said, *"I hope my old man doesn't find out about this."*

"How come?" Fargus said, struggling up onto one elbow.

"He'll jerk me out of school," Weathermore said. He heard his own voice go flat, tired and sad now rather than desperate.

"Guys fight all the time," Fargus said.

"Not me. I can't afford to."

"How come?" Fargus blinked.

Weathermore paused. *"Say,"* he said, smiling and looking up. *"You think there's any chance your head is really hurt?"*

"Nah. Been beaned worse with baseballs," Fargus said.

"Well, look. Let's get outa here."

"Will they let us?"

"No, but there's a window," Weathermore said.

"Suits me," said Fargus, and they both got quietly out of bed.

Weathermore expertly removed the screen and set it on the bed. Then he went first, jumping the six feet to the alley below. *"Jump,"* he whispered back up to Fargus. *"I'll catch you."*

Fargus shook his head, but Weathermore could see that he was having trouble finding the ledge. Then he slipped, and Weathermore caught him. Weathermore set Fargus on his feet, and they began walking up the alley.

"Look, man," Weathermore said, *"you got no idea how much I appreciate you leavin'."*

"What's the problem?" Fargus said.

Weathermore was walking slowly with his head down. He hoped that Fargus couldn't tell from the sound of his breathing how badly his ribs hurt. "Nothin', man. I'm just glad my old man's not gettin' no bill is all."

"You're talking funny," Fargus said.

"That's right, man." Weathermore suddenly stopped and sat on the curb. He was crying.

"Look," Fargus said. "Are you hurt?"

"Nah."

Fargus sat down beside him. "Well, look, what the hell's going on?"

"You won't tell nobody?"

"No."

"Cause if you do, I'm screwed." Weathermore was looking Fargus in the face.

"Are you hurt?" Fargus said.

"Unless that's what you call bein' a nigger," Weathermore said.

"A nigger? You don't look—or maybe you do."

"Well, you don't have to get snotty about it," Weathermore said. "It's just one sixteenth."

"Sure," Fargus said.

"But my old man's an eighth, and he looks it, and if anybody ever finds out I'm one, he'll beat the dog shit out of me."

Fargus thought for a moment. "Your old man must be rich, huh," he said.

"Owns a steamship," Weathermore said.

"Out of New Orleans?"

Weathermore nodded. "You don't hate me?" he said.

"No."

"And you won't tell anybody?"

"No."

"You may be the only friend I have here," Weathermore said.

Fargus thought again for a long moment. "What about your mother?" he asked.

"She paid my old man for a stud—before he got the steamship. Then she wouldn't have no nigger baby, and she left my old man with me."

"Oh," Fargus had said; the shape of the word had lingered in his mouth.

19

3

It was a gray sort of a late afternoon. There was no sunset in Fargus' west window, no irregularity anywhere in the overcast dome which followed above the Cessna. The showers had vanished. Fargus liked the vague hint of movement and vibration which seeped into the insulated cabin. If it didn't take his mind off the Fargus technique—and Weathermore hadn't been able to do that either— it at least made it seem distant and harmless. Fargus gazed out the window. The Fargus technique seemed like something that might be going on in one of the tiny houses passing silently beneath them, something barely relieved against the dark earth below.

Out of the west the Mississippi River was sidling slowly into place directly beneath the plane—a place to set down if the weather got too bad. It was backed up full and high from the spring rain. Down in the heart of the dark earth, it seemed to catch and hold the sky's failing light. Fargus felt his own mood change. For an instant the cold light gave him an ominous feeling. For a second, it was as if the river were a giant, constipated water moccasin sprawled across the land. Then the feeling passed. He looked away into the still, gray sky, thinking of Alice. He wondered if she was still mad.

He hoped not, because if she was, her eyes would be hurting and then she wouldn't even enjoy the kids. And I want her to enjoy that, he thought, if she's gonna be down there, she at least ought to get to enjoy it. But I swear, I can't think of what she must tell herself about her life if she can't think of anything better to do than worry about the kids. Fargus shook his head and rubbed his own eyes. No responsibilities in the world with them married and gone. She could do anything she wanted. And what does she do? Sits home and worries about everybody else. Can't even leave the lab two hours early without getting her upset.

That day I left the lab early, I guess, was the day it really began to fall apart. I went to work as usual. The thing was all but ready to be tested on people. It worked, too, as long as you weren't trying to get pregnant, because sperm can't live in an acid environment either—but I don't want to go into that now. Let's just say it worked. It would have

20

worked, that is, but I kept sweating and losing the train of what I was doing. After two solid years, I was forgetting my procedures. I stepped out, told the technician I was sick, and went home.

I expected Alice to meet me at the door with her face full of questions, but it was Mrs. Wellbourne, the next-door neighbor, who got to me first.

"Well," she cackled, "it certainly is a switch to see you home this time of day."

I nodded, almost running, and escaped inside. But Alice wasn't there, not that I wanted to see her, but that wasn't reassuring. I tiptoed upstairs, peeking around into doorways.

She was sitting in the study with her knitting on her lap, but she wasn't even knitting. I had to go in; it would have been even more unnatural not to. The TV was on one of those afternoon kid shows, but the volume was off. The screen cast a faint glow across the shadowed carpet.

"Hello, sweetheart." I sat across from her in my chair. "Eyes hurting real bad today?"

"Awful. You home for the day?"

"Yeah," I said. "I'm a little tired. Here"—I jumped back up—"let me get your pills. Have you taken one?"

"No, I was just fixing to." She was really putting on the suffering act. I didn't want to watch it. I went to get the pills.

"Here, darling." She took one and swallowed it and drank the water, big-eyed and wet-faced like a goldfish.

"Thank you," she said quietly.

"Where's your dog?" I said. She has had her own dog ever since the collie died, a toy poodle that Mrs. Wellbourne gave her to keep her company.

"I put him outside. He was making me nervous."

"Poor dear," I said.

"You know, I've been thinking," she said, suddenly talking fast. "Maybe I want to get rid of him. He's a good dog, but I don't think I need him. Maybe it would be better to give him to somebody who has a farm where he could get some exercise. Dogs like that need a lot of exercise." By the time she finished, she was sitting bolt upright.

"Well, whatever you say," I said. "I kind of hoped you'd enjoy him."

21

"I think I want you to take him for me," she said, sinking back into her sofa. "Will you do it soon?"

"Sure."

"It's not good to wait, once you decide something like that."

"No. Sure."

"Thank you."

She smiled.

I crossed my legs.

She looked away.

"How are your eyes?"

"They're all right."

"Anything else wrong?"

"No. I suppose not." She spoke very quietly.

"I was tired today, so I left early. Windy days used to make you tired," I said.

"Yes."

"You know, it won't be long till spring."

"That will be nice. This winter's seemed long."

"Terribly." I closed my eyes and touched my fingertips together.

"It'll be good to have flowers."

"Sure," I said.

"Uh-huh," she said.

"Honey, what's wrong?" I said.

"Nothing."

"There is too."

"Oh, it's nothing," she said in her own inimitable way.

"It is."

"Well, what about you?" she said. "You don't seem so good either."

"I'm tired."

"I am too."

"You haven't done anything."

"Well, maybe that's what I'm tired of."

"Well, why don't you do something?"

"There's nobody to do it with."

"Make some friends. Go to the bridge club."

"I don't like bridge."

"Oh, my God!" I said, then immediately regretted it.

"Henry, please don't get mad," she said, hurt. "Don't take the Lord's name in vain."

"Sure. I'm sorry."

"Henry, I'm so depressed."

"It's just your hormones, darling. Try and think above it."

"Oh, I'm so tired of being just a case. Anytime I feel bad you just explain it away as if it was nothing."

"Well, darling, what do you want to do?"

"I want to be near the kids. I want us to retire and move to Florida and be near Cindy and Freddy."

"No!"

"Why not? You said yourself we've got more money than we'll ever spend. You aren't practicing anymore, and you aren't getting any pleasure out of your work."

"What do you mean, not getting any pleasure? What makes you think I'm doing it for pleasure? Maybe I'm trying to accomplish something with my life. Do somebody some good, you know? Is that so inconceivable to you?"

"Well, what about me? Aren't I somebody?"

"Yes, but you're supposed to be able to take care of yourself," I shot back.

"One time I could, Henry."

"Listen," I said. "That research is my life. It's my whole reputation."

"Well, why? You don't enjoy it anymore."

"That's not true. I'm just tired. I need a vacation. I do enjoy it, and I'm not quitting."

"Then let's take a vacation," she said, suddenly excited, "to Florida and see the kids."

"You go to Florida," I said, staring at the TV. "I don't want to. I want to go fishing. I don't want to go pester the kids."

"Oh, Henry, let's please don't fight. We haven't fought in so long. I don't think I can stand it if we have a fight. I think I'll just go into hysterics."

"Okay, okay. I'm just tired. I just need a vacation. You go to Florida, and I'll go fishing."

"Yes, darling, yes. That'll be good."

"Yes."

23

She straightened her knitting.
I recrossed my knees.
"I love you," she said.
"I love you."
She got up and turned up the TV sound.
"I think I'll go up and do some reading," I said.
She smiled, and I left.
So I didn't really think she'd go. And I don't think she thought she would either. She just wanted to hold that going to Florida against me, so I wouldn't go off fishing with Arnold. She just couldn't stand the idea of me going off fishing and leaving her by herself there at the house.

"Arnold," Fargus said, "the problem with you is you just don't understand women."

"Hah!" Weathermore said. "The problem with you is you try!"

"Oh?"

"Sure," Weathermore said, "isn't that what a gynecologist is supposed to do?"

"Well," said Fargus, "I never had quite thought of it that way."

"Damn right," said Weathermore, "and I can tell you right now why the Fargus technique is giving you fits."

"Indeed?"

"You," he said, "are attempting to comprehend the incomprehensible. You are attempting to manipulate the one organ, the one entity in the entire universe which defies the law of cause and effect."

"You're just bitter," Fargus teased. "You've got a case of vagina envy."

"That's all right," Weathermore said. "I'd rather have vagina envy any day than a wife."

My friend Arnold Weathermore! Anyhow the next morning I got up and went back to the hospital. The first thing I did was go to the switchboard and have the girl start trying to call Arnold from St. Louis. Then I went to the cafeteria and got some coffee. I was in no hurry to go back upstairs.

Always in the past we'd gone to Canada on our fishing trips, but it

24

was too early in the year for that now. We'd go in the Gulf this time, fly out to Chandeleur Islands, and fish in the surf for big redfish and speckled trout. Last week I had seen in the paper where a party of three caught over two hundred pounds. If we camped and stayed a week, Lord knows what we ought to get. Arnold would love it too, once I got him out there. He claims a great disdain for saltwater fishing, claims it requires no finesse. He fishes for nothing but stream trout. Great purist. He uses only these two hundred dollar, split-bamboo rods from Abercrombie and Fitch. Great connoisseur. He's hell's own one for finesse, purism, and connoisseurship. But he'll forget it first time he gets a ten-pound red on. Better be tough though, or he won't go. Just tell him we're going. Just be here, that's all, you half-black ape.

I stirred the coffee slowly and sipped it, avoiding looking at the clock. There was hardly anyone here when I came in, and now the place was nearly full. Just one couple's been here the whole time. Look like they might have been here all night. Grandchild on the way? No, they're too far gone. More like on the way out from their looks. But it's always like that with couples. If they come by themselves, they don't have to act sad or worried the whole time. They can drink coffee and read magazines, get their minds on something else. But when you come with your wife, both of you know why you're there. You can't forget it because it's between you, and neither one of you can control it. That pair really looked like they'd had it though. I'm sick of hospitals. This morning I had started smelling the ether again. And I'm sick of things getting between me and Alice that neither of us can control.

Then the switchboard paged me, and I talked to Arnold.

I got another cup of coffee to go and took the fast elevator up. The fast elevator splashed coffee all over me when it stopped, and I threw the cup away outside the lab. They make coffee in the lab, but they drip it in a two-liter flask for a joke. I used to think it was funny, but now it makes me sick. I went in the office and slammed the door. The place was a wreck. I never noticed that when I was really going on the Far-gus technique. You don't when you're really going on something like that. You don't care about anything like that. You lock the door and won't let a maid in, and you're going so hard you don't care how many times you miss the wastebasket. But the second you stop believing in it it jumps out at you. I sat down and started going like crazy trying to clean it up. Then, about the time I got it straight enough to start won *dering what to do next, a terrific peal of thunder came rattling through the walls.*

It was good to have the rain outside and the wind singing in the heating vents and to be going fishing, but now I did need to do some work. No matter what, you just can't quit working without any reason. Get a cold or something, or go fishing, or take a day off now and then, but when you just quit because—well, who knows why?—anyway that's when it really goes bad. So I started writing up some notes for when I would compose the questionnaire for all the doctors who would try out my technique. Then the intercom crackled: "Dr. Fargus, Line 23 please. An emergency." I took it in the lab.

"Henry?" Alice. Her voice was wet with the pills.

"What is it, honey?"

"Henry—do you love me?"

"Of course."

"Something just happened." I could hear her turn her face away from the mouthpiece.

"What was it, darling?"

"The dog. You said you were going to get rid of it for me."

"Yes?"

"You didn't."

"I'll get rid of it this afternoon." I could hear her turn away from the mouthpiece again. She was gasping. "What is it? What's happened?"

"Nothing."

"What is it?"

"Well, I was just sitting there. In the den, you know?"

"Yes."

"And this baby commercial came on. Ivory Snow, with a little naked baby."

"Yes."

"I just wanted to touch the baby so bad, you know? Oh, I don't know." She'd had way too many pills, but not enough to really hurt her.

"Yes."

"Anyway, I picked up the dog and was rocking it. I was watching Concentration and rocking the dog."

"Uh-huh."

"And then—Henry, do you love me?"

26

"Yes."

"And then I looked down—and—I was holding the dog real tight, Henry. And my lips were saying 'baby, baby,' and the dog was licking my breasts."

Oh, my God!—I didn't say it out loud.

"Henry, I screamed. I threw the dog on the floor, and I screamed, and the dog ran away yelling, and then I had to come call you to come get the dog."

"Alice!"

"Henry, you said you'd take the dog away!"

"I'll take the dog away this afternoon."

"Now, Henry!"

"Alice, put the dog out—"

"No—"

"Put the dog outside and don't let it back in. And then you go to bed, and you can sleep the whole rest of the day."

"Henry, no!"

"Alice, I'll see you this afternoon." I hung up.

I waited a second to see if she would call back. She didn't, and I took that as a sign that she wasn't going to do anything desperate. She'd sure call twice before she did anything. Then I went back to work.

I needed to work. I stared at the forms I'd been typing and pecked out a line. But I couldn't hit the right keys.

I wanted to get out of here. I wanted to walk out in the cold Gulf of Mexico and catch a sixty-pound redfish and eat it right there on the beach and never tell anybody about it. I didn't want to work either, but I had to.

Just outside my door there was a window. The storm had leveled itself out into a good one now. No more fireworks, and the wind was strong and constant. I tried to lose my thoughts in the sound of the rain. But something had to keep going through my head. It couldn't be fishing because my conscience screamed. And I would have rather done anything than think about working. So I thought about Alice wanting to go visit the kids. Why can't she think of anything better to do with her life than plague them? I love you, she said when the crisis was avoided. You better, prune. You don't know what you've got.

27

Then something happened just as Weathermore was turning to speak that both men understood. Their ears popped, the motor raced, and for an instant it was as though the Cessna had lost all grip on the air. When the instant passed, a gust hit them from Fargus' side of the plane like a wet, heavy mallet. They were staring at each other now.

"The pressure," Weathermore said.

"No kidding?"

Weathermore didn't smile. He craned his neck, peering back out the side window. "God," he said, "how did that sneak up on us?"

Fargus turned and looked. Out of the north a cobalt thunderhead was bearing down on them like a wave laced with fire. It was racing before the wind with massive shapes bursting and re-forming within a single lightning flash. The sky around it was yellowish green in the last of the sunlight. Fargus looked away. Weathermore pushed the throttle wide open. "Gonna run from it, huh?" Fargus asked.

Weathermore nodded without turning. His teeth covered his lower lip.

Fargus stared ahead through the windshield. He relaxed. There was not a thing he could do. He relaxed again.

So I stood in the hospital window until the rain slacked off. Then I went and locked the closet. I headed for the exit as fast as I could, thinking of one thing—a big stiff drink just as quick as I could get home.

The instant I hit the door I could tell something was wrong. It came from little things: a coffee cup left out in the kitchen, a newspaper left unopened. But when you live with Alice this long, little signs become positive proof. Then when Losla May, the maid, ran past the door through the hall without even seeing me I was sure. I never like to rush in on this sort of thing. I sauntered slowly upstairs, preparing myself mentally in case it was a crisis. Alice was in her room, and I stuck my head in the door. "Hi," I said, "I'm home."

"Oh, good! I was just fixing to call you back."

"You don't even want to know why I'm home?" Her suitcase was out, the bureau drawers open, and several dresses folded across the bed.

"Of course, dear." She struck back with a wet peck below my eye,

then stood still before me with her arms full of clothes, pill-grinning hugely. "What happened?"

"I'm depressed," I said, "and I was going to take care of the dog."

"Oh." She leapt back into motion. "Well, that'll all be taken care of when you and Arnold Weathermore go fishing. But I needed you to make sure you could be here when Losla May gets back to take her home. I have to catch the twelve-fifty plane for Tampa."

"You what?"

She stopped packing instantly, feigning shock. This was what was wrong. She could have managed it over the phone, but as it was, I'd walked right into it.

"I called Cindy this morning and told her how I was feeling and how you didn't have time to help me. And Jack is going on a business trip starting tomorrow, and she said she'd be glad to have me come stay with her and the children while he's gone. I've already made reservations."

"You've already made them, huh?"

"Yes, dear."

"And you weren't afraid that might cause a crisis."

"Well, of course not, dear. We already discussed it. You were going fishing and—"

"So you just went ahead and made the reservations."

"Well, Jack was leaving tomorrow."

"Okay," I said. "Go. Hear?" I walked to the door and turned back. "You just go!" I stalked out and down the hall to my study.

I sat in my soft chair, nursing the Wild Turkey. Fine whiskey! I thought I'd leave about three empty bottles around for Alice to find when she got home. Fix her! Wanted me to tell her not to go because then I'd have to promise not to go fishing. End up both going to Florida in June. Go. Hear? Go, bitch. Go, simpering hypochondriac. Go, doily knitter. Make a pilgrimage to the shrine of the Great God Grandbaby.

And she was going. I heard Losla May go into her room and carry the bags out. Then I heard the Cadillac start. Losla May must be gonna bring the car back from the airport. Hafta do that about the bottles. When did she say she'd be back? Jack gonna be gone a week. He'll run her off quick enough when he gets back. Mother-in-law! Hafta be sure to give the maid the week off if Alice didn't think to. I bet she didn't. She didn't think she was going. Her mind did. She has *the tickets all right. But she didn't feel like she was. That was a real crisis, and she wouldn't have thought she could go through with it.*

Damned fine whiskey! Forget it. She's gone. Poor thing's scared to death of airplanes. Sad is what it is. Critics used to jump on Faulkner for not "appreciating female concupiscence." Shows how much they know about women. Because there's not really any such thing. Girls aren't raised for it. Raised for doily knitters. What'd Faulkner call it? Look it up. Where's damn book? Here. Abslumabslum. *Ellen Colfiel'. Goddam it, I know I underlined it. Here—"butterfly summer!" Hafta have that butterfly summer. Raised for nothin' but that, and when that's over, they have it for their daughters, and when that's over, they worship grandbabies. Critics don't know a goddam thing about Faulkner or women or anything.*

Faulkner's greatest writer ever lived. I love Mississippi, goddam it. I don't mean I like it. I mean it's a stupid, backward, naive, underdeveloped fen of prejudice and injustice, Arnold Weathermore. You hear that, you half-black son-of-a-bitch? And I love Alice, too, you irresponsible bachelor—I didn't say "like." And you have that airplane here on time, too, or I may kill myself. You hear that, Alice? Bitch? You think you're bored now. Butterfly!

I emptied the bottle, put it in the drawer for safekeeping. Then I went downstairs and took the Volkswagen to the liquor store for two more of the same. Back home again, I set the two bottles on the kitchen table. No need to stay in the study now. I poured a glass half full and started sipping it straight.

Then I heard the Cadillac pull into the driveway. I heard Losla May tripping up the back steps, two at a time. She dodged inside the door and put the keys down in front of me. She just stood there, holding her purse, with her apron off, looking at me like a combination of a shy schoolgirl and a poodle wanting to go for a walk. She's twenty-four, married to a hellacious-looking buck about twice her age. But she's been working for us since she was fourteen, and she still acts fourteen around me.

"Lawsamussy, Doct Fa'gus," she says, "you look like you plannin' on some tall drankin' while Mrs. Alice gone."

I grunted.

"Uh"—she averted her eyes—"Doct Fa'gus, has you got ennythang

lef' fo' me t'do? Mrs. Alice says you just take me on home early. That is, course, if you ain't got nothin' lef' fo' me to do."

"No, I don't have anything. If you'll just sit down over there and let me finish this drink."

"Well, Mrs. Alice say you take me right on home."

I looked at my watch. "Let me see. It's ten till two. You get off at three thirty. Did she give you the week off while she's gone?"

"Nah suh!" Her eyes bugged.

"Sit down."

"Yassuh!"

"Here." I reached her a juice glass and poured her about a third as much whiskey as I had. "You might as well—while you wait."

"Lawd! That expensive stuff?" She closed her eyes and took a big gulp, nearly convulsed as she swallowed, then looked at me, bug-eyed, blinking her false eyelashes and shaking her legs under the table. "Lawd have mussy. That is some whiskey."

"She didn't say when she'd be back, did she?"

"Uh—uh—she say she don't know." She averted her eyes again.

"She said not to tell me."

"Nawsuh. Nawsuh."

"Do you want next week off?"

"But, yassuh, Doct Fa'gus, but she say—lawsamussy, she fiah me if I tell."

"She'll never know it. Do you want next week off—with pay—or do you want to work?"

"O lawd, what I'm s'posed to do? I wish y'all'd git together on these thangs."

I concentrated on the whiskey.

"She say she be back nex' Tuesday, one week f'om today."

"Good," I smiled. I'd still be gone. "Well, look. You're not supposed to pick her up at the airport or anything, are you?"

"Yassuh, I is."

"Well, you get sick that day, see? Whatever time you're supposed to pick her up, you call the airport and have her paged and tell her you're sick in bed. You come back to work Wednesday. Not before, understand?"

"Yassuh."

31

"You do it all right, and it's an extra day's pay. You goof, and you're fired."

"Yassuh, yassuh, Doct Fa'gus. I do it all right."

It was a sight to watch her drink. She'd hold the glass under her nose, sniff it, then close her eyes and take a huge gulp, slam the glass back on the table and shudder all over, then look across at me, blinking her false eyelashes and knocking her knees together under the table.

"You like the whiskey?" I asked.

"Lawsamussy, that is some pow'ful stuff."

"What do you usually drink?"

"I likes Pussycats." She took another gulp, and her eyes were watering, ruining her lashes.

"Oh, yeah. That new mix stuff. You put whiskey in that, don't you?" She giggled.

"Don't you?" I said.

"Well, ya see, I ain't had but one pitcher so I don't really know."

"Pitcher? That's some pow'ful drankin'."

She nodded, finished what I had poured her, then reached for the bottle and filled her glass. "Yassuh," she grinned.

"Help yourself," I said as she took her first sip. I took a sip of my own.

She grinned, gulped, and shuddered.

"You must really like this stuff," I said.

"Well, see, dis the first I ever had."

"First you ever had? What about the Pussycat?"

She giggled again. "Well, ya see, dey gimme dis whole in-vellup full of that there wachacallit mix stuff when I's down to the grocery store one day aftah work. I's all tiahed out, so when I got home I got me a glass o' watah and put in a teaspoonful and I thought I'd have me a little taste fore my man come home"—giggle—"So I drunk that glass an' didn' feel nothin'—I figgahed I ain't had enough, so I made me anothah one, an' I still didn' feel nothin'. Well, I says to m'self, dis here is the weakest stuff I have evah had. But I's determined I's goan get some elevation from my misery, so I got me a whole pitchah full of watah an' I poured the whole in-vellup in it an' sat down an' started drankin'. Well, long bout then my man come in the doah, an' he say, lawsamussy, woman, what you drankin'? An' I says, Pussycat! An' he say, you

mean you done took an' spent yo' paycheck on liquah? Well sir, I
knowed right then and theah what I'd done wrong. An' fu'thah moah I
knowed I was in a pree-dicament. Cause if I tell him I done bought liquah with my paycheck he's goan beat the blazes outah me. But if I
tell him de truf about what I done, I goan be the laughin' stock of Em-
minence Street fo' years to come. So I give out with a big hiccup and
says, yassuh, that's what I done fo' sho'. I done drank me a gallon o'
thunda'bold wine in this here Pussycat." She giggled some more,
slapped her knee, and had another gulp.

"Lord," I said. "Then did he beat you up?"

"He sho' beat the blazes outah me."

I was drunk, and the picture came in a flash: the black flesh stripped
to the waist and the huge buck Negro standing over her with a belt, red
on black. I stared at her until it went away. "Does he do that very
often?"

"He sho' do."

"Jesus, why don't you leave him?" Red on black.

"He sho' beat me up if I do that."

"You mean you can't call the cops or something?"

"Now what I'm gonna do somethin' like that for?"

"You mean you don't mind?"

"Well, sho', I minds it at de time, but he do it to make me respect
him. He don' gimme a good hidin' but bout once a week I's liable to be
cuttin' out with evah man in town."

Red on black. Red on black.

She took another big gulp, but this time she didn't look at me. She
stared at the glass, and her eyes were very wet.

"Here," I said. "Have some more."

She pushed the glass toward me, but said nothing. My eyes were wet,
too. Finally she said, "Now you thank I'm just a low-rate niggah an'
them's just low-rate niggah ways." Another gulp without looking at
me.

"No," I said, "no, I don't. Not at all."

"You don't?"

"No, really. Lots of times I think it would be better if I beat Mrs.
Alice."

"It would." She nodded. "Woman needs that if she's gonna respect a
man. She sho' does."

33

"She does," I said.

Then she stuck her face out at me. "But you don't ebm know how ta beat nobody, Doct Fa'gus. I can tell dat by watching you."

"What do you mean?" I said. "I'll beat the blazes outa you."

When she looked at me, her eyes were very wet. She was trembling. "But youah a white man." She said it very softly but very distinctly.

"That's right," I said.

Then she said no more. She knew already what to do, and I picked it up. She took off her blouse, and I took off my belt, and she never screamed—There was only a high doleful singsong throughout while she swayed and rocked under the blows, and then we were together on the floor, and then it was over, and at first I couldn't bear to look at her.

But she made me look by the tone in her voice, and once I looked, I stared in fascination. "He goan kill us bofe." Still the high, doleful singsong, still swaying on the kitchen floor. "My man goan kill us bofe. O lawd, ha-a-a-ve mussy, my man goan kill us bofe."

"Oh, God," I said. "What's his name?"

"Blue," she said. "Blue Jesus, an' he goan kill us bofe."

"Oh, my God," I said. "Oh, my God."

As soon as I could think, I gave her fifty-three dollars—all the cash I had. I called a colored taxi for her, and she left.

The rain came mixed with hail, crackling against the Plexiglas windshield. The Cessna, clawing for a prop-hold in the outraged air, reminded Fargus of a car trying to cross quicksand. The light came in dizzying flashes from behind. For a while Fargus tried holding onto the seat to keep from bouncing around so much, but then he let go and let himself be bounced. He didn't get jarred as badly if he didn't try to hold on. In the bouncing plane, with the inconstant, sick-colored light, Fargus felt nauseated. He wasn't afraid. He understood their situation, pictured what might happen, and still wasn't afraid. And in a way, this added to the nausea. He turned to the window again, shielding his forehead with his hand. Arnold was losing his race with the storm.

4

Weathermore tightened his seatbelt and bored the Cessna into darkness. It was black dark now except for the lightning. He could see nothing anywhere, except for the wingtip lights and the glow of the instruments. At irregular intervals of five to thirty seconds, gusts were slamming the airplane so hard that he had to hold his neck stiff to keep from bashing his head against something.

He glanced at Fargus. Fargus was bouncing around, gazing at him. Surely Fargus knew that it wasn't his flying. Fargus had been a pilot; he knew nobody could fly a goddam Cessna with floats on it in this kind of wind. Weathermore thought a filthy expletive and concentrated on the black windshield.

"So what's the deal on you alluvasudden trying to tell everybody you're nigger?" Fargus said suddenly, but calmly. "Gonna try and fight the *bête noire* out in the open or what?"

This irritated Weathermore. How could Fargus talk like that at a time like this? "Actually, it was never anything more than a matter of practicality that kept me from saying it in the first place." Weathermore spat.

"Uh-huh. So as soon as you decide to make a clean breast of things, you run out and join the NAACP and the Black Panthers. God knows what all else. Come sporting a hair-do no self-respecting agitator would wear to a policeman's ball."

"What's the matter?" Weathermore shot back. "Don't you have any conscience—any sense of social injustice?"

"That's right," Fargus said, "and as I recall, back among the hallowed halls of all-white ivy at Ole Miss, your alma mater and mine —remember?—there was no one yelled any louder when some nigger would get out of line." Fargus chuckled.

"Well, just fuck you, hear?" Weathermore shot back. "Just shut up."

The wind was tossing the airplane around like a paper wad, so hard that half the time Weathermore couldn't even tell up from down. The rain cut visibility to zero even in the very frequent flashes of lightning. The sound of it on the outside of the plane was like some stupendous, grinding engine. And Fargus didn't even care!

"Arnold," Fargus said, "are you gonna be able to set this thing down?"

"Well, if it hadn't been for this pig wallow of a state we're in, I'd of never taken off in it to begin with."

Weathermore shielded his head from a series of heavy bumps. When they passed, lightning flared all around and left him flash-blind.

"Arnold," Fargus said, "can you see anything at all?"

"No!" he screamed. The lightning flashed again, and he could see Fargus' face. It was quiet, passive, slightly green from the dash lights.

Weathermore could feel his own face. His eyes felt huge in the darkness. His cheeks were sucked between his teeth. He felt that it was the face of a maniac.

"You mean," Fargus said, "that means, we might be like not much above tree level or something?"

"Right." Nodding. He said it very quietly and was breathing very heavily.

There came a relatively smooth space, and he remembered the look on Fargus' face. There was something about it, but it wasn't fear. Embarrassment about the trip? Not Fargus. But it was something, something close to *amor fati,* something like highly interested resignation. What was Fargus thinking about him?

"What about the radio?" Fargus said.

"You can try it," he said. "I've got to keep this thing into the wind. You probably won't get anything though with all this lightning interference."

Fargus picked up the microphone. "This is NC–13725 to anybody. . . . We're in trouble." There was nothing but static, and you could hardly hear that above the wind and the rain.

"Oh, for Chris' sake! Damn state doesn't even have an airport," Weathermore said.

Then the lightning flared again, and Fargus suddenly had his face glued to the window. "Arnold," he said, cushioning his head against the glass. Weathermore didn't answer. Then it came again, and Weathermore saw it too, a reflection of water. "Water," Fargus shouted. "It must be the river. You could land it in the river."

Weathermore craned his neck. "In this stuff who could land it anywhere?" he shouted. He hoped to God Fargus didn't think he ought to just be able to set it down there like nothing. "Are you sure?" Weathermore said. "Where?"

"Down there! Back there! You have to wait for the lightning. Can't you turn on the landing lights? Can't you go back there and look?"

"Back where?" Weathermore shouted. "I don't even know where we are."

But then the lightning came again, and he could see it—water and massive stands of trees.

"Can you land it there?" Fargus shouted.

"I don't know. I can't tell how much is there. Is it the river?"

"I don't know. It looked like it. Can't you turn on the lights and go back and look?"

Weathermore was silent for long seconds. Then he muttered under his breath, "Motherfucking state," and said without shouting, "I guess we've got to try."

He tried to pour his attention through the windshield. He leaned his body into the turn, and he could feel the tortuous stress as the wings came flat against the wind. He shoved the throttle wide, trying to get enough airspeed to control the plane against the gusts. Weathermore felt the total hostility of the air, the only thing keeping him up. He felt the g's draw blood out of his face. The lightning flared again, and he could see the water out in front, as though the light were tantalizing him with it, dangling it in front of him, then making it disappear. There's the water, nigger; now see if you can hit it with your airplane.

In the next flash, he didn't even look for the water. A twister was ripping through the trees about two miles ahead. Weathermore's stomach turned to ice. The lightning seemed to last for hours. The twister moved with a morbidly fascinating grace, serpentine and seductive. He wondered if Fargus saw it. When the next flash came, it was gone.

He switched on the landing lights. Then there came a bad second when a tail wind overran the plane. He felt the lift vanish, the Cessna falling like a shot bird. But then the prop bit again, and there was a terrific noise, like ripping canvas. His controls came back.

He could see the trees in the landing lights. Too little altitude, not over a hundred yards. The speed seemed terrific. Although the light was constant, things appeared for only a split second. Seconds passed. A minute. The wind was slamming the plane with twice the force that it had when they were traveling against it. Two minutes. No water.

"I'm gonna have to pull up," he shouted desperately. "We're not a hundred feet over those trees."

"Wait! There it is, off to the right."

"Where, for God's sake?"

"Right there. Right there!—For Chris' sake—turn!—Point the lights to the right—there, between those trees."

"Oh, shit. I don't know if we can make it this pass. I still don't know if it's big enough. Could you tell if it was the river?"

"No. I don't know. You've got to get closer."

So he leaned into the controls again, and the ripping canvas sound came again, even above the rain. They were barely above treetop level, bucking like a roller coaster, but now the water was squarely in the landing lights. He still couldn't tell if it was the river, but it was big. It was big enough. If he could get at it from the right direction. If he didn't hit a tree. If the wings didn't blow off first.

He glanced at Fargus. Fargus was shielding his head from the bucking, not even looking at the window. He could see it all over Fargus' green face—Arnold's airplane, Arnold's job to get it down. Fargus wasn't even paying any attention anymore!

He passed over the water and got one long look at it in about a five-second flash of lightning. Then he was over the trees again. At least he had seen it. He was low enough to judge where he was in relation to it. There was one way, only one way, that he could come down on it. He swung the Cessna into another turn, maneuvering it like a fighter plane. He set the airplane and himself. Then came the long, nerve-wracking, terrifying power glide into what looked like black nothingness, guided only by the faint reflections, far ahead in the lightning.

Trees loomed and disappeared beneath him. The top of a tall pine passed above eye level. Once he would have sworn he felt branches brush a pontoon. Neither of them spoke.

As soon as he was over the water, he knew it wasn't the river because he could see the end of what would have had to be the channel. But he set the flaps and came back on the throttle, set a dying note in the engine, and the airplane sank, touched, skipped, touched without skipping.

And then there was another terrific crash—a log. The airplane hooked wildly to the right and skewed up onto one pontoon, then righted and went on, clipping through brush and half-submerged tree limbs until it finally slowed. It slowed even more, and they were still in the middle of the whipping lake and the right side of the plane was dipping.

"It's sinking," Weathermore shouted. "The right side's going down."

The land was maybe two hundred yards to the right. He gunned the engine and fought the controls against the sinking pontoon. The airplane veered wildly to the right, and then he had the pontoon up and planing, clipping through more brush and logs, and then, for no reason, it went down again, and the airplane reared over onto its right side and spun in a complete circle, then righted again, and he gunned the engine. He raced for the shore until about sixty feet out everything slammed to a stop. He killed the engine.

For a long time, neither spoke. The airplane was tilting slowly over onto its side as the pontoon filled. Then it must have hit the bottom. It stopped. Except for the lightning, the blackness was total. Then Weathermore opened the door. He leaned out the side and vomited.

"Are you all right?" Fargus said.

"Just fuck it," he said. "Just fuck you and this whole goddam state. Just fuck it."

Part II

It was one of those oxbow lakes that are all along the Mississippi, albeit a very deserted one. Some of these lakes used to be a part of the channel before some cataclysm changed the river's course. Some are just giant old sloughs that flow when the river is high. But nearly all of them look just like the river itself, except that there is no current. This one was a desolate and lonely spot.

In the shallow water around the lake's edge stood giant cypresses, so tall and old and so long undisturbed that if you thought of them at all you had to think that they must be surprised at the wounded, stiff-winged bird sheltering in their circle. They were quiet, patient trees, even in the wind. Their bones and the bones of their predecessors littered the lake about their trunks.

The Cessna had grounded one pontoon on a shallow bar near the inside of the bow. In the night, after the storm, Fargus and Weathermore had waded ashore and made a camp on what is known as the island side of such a lake. This means that there is no overland route off the island, that on the other side of the land is the river itself, and that at either end of the lake are heavy stands of cypress and willow growing in quick, blue-gumbo mud and riddled with fast-flowing chutes connecting to the river.

But the storm had left the sky absolutely clear of clouds. In the dawn before the morning breeze arose, the tiny leaves and cypress fronds seemed fairly to tingle with droplets of water in the new light. It was a precious day of early spring.

1

When I woke, Arnold wasn't in his sleeping bag. I hoisted myself out of my own, then saw him down by the airplane, up to his knees in the water, doing something around the sunken float. I stood up and yawned hugely, scratching a place where a mosquito had bitten me in the night.

The four duffel bags were scattered around the sleeping bags where we had dumped them last night. It was a high, sandy bluff, the driest place we could find in the dark. I watched Arnold for a second; he was preoccupied with the plane. Then I went to the nearest pack and began scrounging around inside. I found a pipe, then stole some of Arnold's expensive tobacco out of one of his packs. I rolled up my sleeping bag, then sat down against it to awaken with a smoke.

Directly below me a family of beavers was engaged in felling a cluster of small cypress saplings. When one of them saw me, he slapped the water with his tail, and sent the eight gray bulges fleeing just below the surface. White cranes were drifting above the far shore, barely visible against the whitish blue of the morning.

Smoking the pipe gave me a strong urge for coffee. Dry wood was hard to find, so I doused a few sticks with gas. It had been a long time since I'd had boiled coffee, and I hunkered by the fire, smoking the pipe and watching it impatiently.

The coffee was right. Leaning against the sleeping bag, I could feel the jungle at my back. Suddenly, and for no apparent reason, I felt as though I'd been sitting on this bluff for a long time. I felt as if I wanted to die.

I sipped the coffee. The coffee was so right.

Then I knew I didn't want to die. If I died, even this would be over. But I felt good knowing that I could die if I needed to. Back in Jackson you could only make a mess. I felt as though I comprehended this, but with my mind I couldn't get it into coherent thoughts. Screw my mind. I looked back out at the lake.

Just below me a black moccasin was drawing his heavy coils up into the branches where the beavers had been foraging. I thought that if I bothered him he would bite me in an instant, and that's a terrible death. I saw a snake-bitten man once when I was an intern. He vomited and screamed for three hours and then died despite the miracles of medicine. He had been bitten in seven places. It must be terribly beautiful to see a snake like that moving fast enough to get a man in seven places. What must it look like to the man?

There are worse ways of dying, though. That's all right, snake, I thought; you keep your fangs, and I'll keep my distance.

The wind was rising, stirring shiny ripplets on the lake. The big, white Cessna was rocking gently on its one good float. It looked like a great, ridiculous, wounded bird. Then I noticed that Arnold was no longer in sight. "Hey, jigaboo!" I yelled.

"What do you want?" He appeared out of the jungle and sat down by the fire without even looking at me. He was shivering from the wet.

"Well, how does it look? Can the dodo bird be resurrected?"

"Maybe," he muttered. He leaned close over the fire. "Can't you build that up a little? I'm freezing."

"Sorry, Mr. Crow. Them's the only dry sticks in these woods, and I hadda soak them down with gasoline."

"Christ," he said. He leaned closer, and his peace symbol dangled over into the flames.

"Hey, man, you gonna burn your necklace." I reached over and swung it around so it hung down his back, and when I did, I saw the pistol holster under his shirt. "Well"—I took it out—"What have we here?"

"When among savages," he said without looking up, "it pays to go armed."

"Oh, man! Black power!" It was one of those cheap German import jobs with paint instead of bluing that are reportedly as danger-

42

ous to the shooter as the shot-at, but it had a big bore. "What caliber?"

He shrugged.

I swung the cylinder out and removed one of the cartridges. "Yipes! Three-fifty-seven Magnum. You didn't want to mess around."

He suddenly turned and snatched it from my hand, sending the cartridge spinning into the dirt. He grabbed the cartridge and shoved it back into the cylinder without wiping it, shoved the gun back into the holster, and turned on me.

"Look," he said, "cut the shit." He suddenly faced me directly. His face was gray, stubble-rough, and splattered with mud. "Now listen, dammit. We're in big trouble, and as far as I'm concerned it was you and everything from your harebrained trip to your pig wallow of a state that got us into it, so I don't want any more crap, see! Now we're gonna have to go to work to get out of this thing, and there's not but one way we can do it, and I don't want any more shit out of you!"

"No, you listen to me," I said. "You can take that notion and do you-know-what with it. It was not me that got us into all this, and if you want me to help you get us out of it, you may calmly explain what you have in mind and then ask me what I think of it."

"Oh, wait a minute."

"No, you wait a minute, you mulatto bastard. I've spent too long listening to you moaning and groaning about your one-sixteenth nigger blood for you to start talking to me that way the second you decide to start admitting to the world that you've got it.

"Now I'm sorry about your trip and your airplane and everything else, and when we get out of here, I'll certainly be glad to help pay to get it fixed. But until that time you can just shut up about it. Do you hear?"

"Oh, crap, I'm sorry," he said. He was rocking back and forth in front of the fire, chattering his teeth twice as hard. He had his hurt-puppy look, the one he always used when I bawled him out. But this was the first time he had ever cut down on me.

I was curious. "Okay, what's your idea?"

"Gimme some of that damn coffee," he said. "I'm freezing to death."

I poured him the coffee and waited while he sugared and creamed it.

"Don't worry about that pontoon. It's insured."

I ignored him.

Finally he said, "There's two possibilities."

"Yes."

"We'll try one of them first because it's the safest."

"And what's that?"

"We make a lever, a big one, out of two logs." He sipped the coffee, suffering magnificently. "We get the short end under the float and prize it up, and then hang onto the long end until all the water drains out. Then, before the thing sinks again, we work like hell and get something under it to prop it up."

"And then?"

"Then we see if by some hook or crook we can patch it so it'll float long enough for us to take off."

"How big's the hole?"

"Aw, it's bent real bad, but the hole's no bigger'n an egg. Anyhow, we may not have to get it completely stopped for it to float long enough to take off."

"What would we use?"

"I don't know. Mud. Rags. Anything just to keep the water out until we can get it going."

"And what if that doesn't work?"

"Whew"—he winced at the thought—"it would be dangerous. But we gotta get out of here."

I poked the fire.

"There's this thing I saw done one time with a boat. This guy had a big ski boat that got a hole knocked in it on the far side of the lake. Him and his buddies got out an' lifted the boat up and propped one side with a stump. Then they took all the ski ropes and tied the boat to a tree, got in and cranked the motor, and when they got it revved up, they cut the rope. Boat was planing off before the water could start running in."

"Wow," I said.

"Damnedest thing I ever saw. But I'd try it before I'd rot right here."

"Why? What's so wrong with this place?"

"Because I'd be buried for a white man by people who'd of lynched me if they knew I was a nigger."

"Well what do you care? What would it matter if you were dead?"

"Look," he said, staring at me in a way that I had never seen before. "I've been thinking a lot about that. My life hasn't been worth shit to me or anybody else. I've just been thinking about that. All my whole life, every time I tried to do anything or get close to anybody I'd think, I couldn't be doing this if people knew I was a nigger. They wouldn't like me if they knew that.

"Oh, I been good at blaming other people for it. Prejudice! My bitch of a mother who wouldn't keep me. But every time I think about dying, I know it's me I got to blame.

"So I say, okay, I fucked up at living, but I'm goan straighten that out by dying. I'm gonna march in every protest they'll let me in, and one of these days some night rider's gonna blow my brains out, and maybe it'll get some attention, and maybe it'll do some good after all."

"God," I said, "I thought for a minute there you were about to wise up. But you're loonier than ever."

Arnold said nothing.

"Hey," I said, "I know what you could do."

"What?"

"When we get out of here you could just stop in Jackson and stay with Alice and me for a day or so, and you could call a press conference and trot out all your honors from Ole Miss and all that and then tell them you were a nigger there while James Meredith was still totin' a cotton sack. Steal all that idiot's thunder."

He pouted for a second longer, then grinned. "Do you remember, Hank," he said tentatively, "that time right after I told you I was part black when we were thinking about joining a fraternity?"

I thought long and hard. "Oh yeah—I think I told you you'd never get in because you already had two black balls against you."

"Right! Right! So we formed our own."

"Ima Delta Niggah."

"And we decided to make you an honorary nigger so you could join."

"Lord have mercy," I said, "and you know I may be the only honorary nigger in the state."

He grinned, nodding. "And then we went out and urinated in that lab flask and mixed it up with a pipette to make ourselves 'piss-brothers' and then poured it in the chancellor's dog's water bowl."

"And the stupid dog drank it!" I said.

"Lord, those were some good times," Arnold said. "I think that was just about the first time in my life I was ever really happy."

"You better not say that too loud," I said. "Somebody's liable to think you've got strange tastes in happiness."

"Let 'em," he said.

"Damn right," I said. "Let 'em."

Arnold stared off in the direction of the horizon.

I poked at the fire.

Then Arnold stared back at me and said very earnestly, "Do you ever wonder why we can't ever feel that way anymore?"

"Well—uh—I always attributed it to the passage of time."

"No, I mean it's more than that, Hank. I don't even feel like the same person I was then—"

"It's your hair, Arnold."

"Wha— Shit, Fargus."

"Take it easy, okay?"

The hurt-puppy look again. "Fargus, I swear, you can be a bastard sometimes. Did you know that?"

I sighed and poured myself some more coffee. "Okay, I guess so. I'm sorry."

No response.

"So when did you stop feeling that way?"

"You don't really want to hear it."

What difference does that make? "Yes, I do."

"It was the night we graduated."

"Where were you? I don't even remember seeing you."

"I was at a nigger hotel. With my ole man."

"What was he doing in a nigger hotel in Oxford?"

"He came for my graduation."

"I see. But he couldn't go to your graduation because everybody would know you were a nigger."

46

"Right. He couldn't even get a room in the white hotel. He had to stay in this place— God, it was a dump. The walls were about ten degrees out of plumb, and it had three stories and looked about twice as high as it was wide. His room was on the top floor."

"So what happened?"

"He drove into town about noon in his Packard and handed me a check for two thousand dollars for a graduation present. Then he wanted to go get something to eat. He made me ride in the back seat so people would think he was the chauffeur, and when we got to the restaurant, he made me go inside and eat and have his food sent out to the car. When I came back out, he'd been hitting the bottle pretty hard, and he had a kind of a grin on his face like he was really teaching me something. Then we went to the campus, and he sat in the car during the whole commencement getting really drunk and listening to the Memphis nigger station on the radio just as loud as it would go. When that was over, we went to the white hotel, and he made me go inside and ask if they knew of any place where my chauffeur could stay. He thought that was the funniest joke of all."

"And that was how you wound up in the nigger hotel," I said.

"That's how we got there," he said, "but that's not how we wound up."

"Oh," I said.

"He bought another bottle from the guy at the hotel and insisted on carrying all the bags up to the room. Then he started calling me Dr. Weathermore and saying Yassuh to me all over the place. He polished my shoes and got shoe polish all over my graduation gown because he wouldn't let me take it off. Pretty soon he just passed out on the floor."

"That's terrible," I said.

Arnold said nothing.

"He didn't live too long after that, did he?" I suggested.

Arnold shook his head.

"What got him? Cirrhosis?"

"No," Arnold said gravely, "he drowned overboard from his ship in the Gulf."

"He fell?"

"Don't shit yourself, Fargus."

I wouldn't think of it.

"He jumped."

"That's very sad," I said. . . .

2

It had been a long time since I had been in Mississippi woods, really big woods. I had forgotten how difficult it is just to move through them. The trees, especially the little saplings with sharp, tough branches low to the ground, are thick enough by themselves. But in among them are giant thickets of blackberry, muscadine, and poison ivy so deep and dense that you can't tell where the ground is. Arnold and I had split up after breakfast to look for some logs for the lever. But even where I could walk, every tree was covered thirty feet up with honeysuckle. I didn't believe that we were going to get out anytime soon.

But I was struck by the unbelievable aliveness of the woods. Despite the difficulty I had in getting a hundred yards back from the lake, everything around me was in motion, furiously struggling, fighting, feeding, breeding in the new spring. The air itself was dark and fecund. Unnumbered northing blackbirds cursed and squawked among the upper branches; then all took wing at once with a soft, heavy sound that was deeper than the wind. I picked up a log, which proved to be hopelessly rotten, and uncovered five baby rabbits. I wondered, If we were going to be here for a while, could you eat baby rabbits? I bet you could. I bet they'd be better than quail. I started to take them back to the fire, but decided that I could come for them anytime if I decided to.

After a while the mosquitoes started attacking, vampires that left a bloody smear when I squashed them. I was getting ready to give up when from the direction of the camp I heard *kawham—kerbloosh—kawham,* then, "Goddam sonofabitch!"

I started running as best I could, stumbling and tripping in the vines, staggering over the uneven ground and bogging in the puddles. Before I got halfway, there came an inarticulate wail, then *kerbloosh—kerbloosh—kerbloosh* again. I struck the shore between the camp and the plane and saw Arnold standing in the water, just out from the camp, with a newly felled log at his feet, frantically reloading the pistol and staring at something in the edge of the water.

"What's going on?" I yelled.

But before he could answer, he had the pistol up again and was raising geysers all over the surface between himself and the shore. *Kerbloosh—kerbloosh* six times until the gun was empty again, and he looked up at me with a face as white as any man's alive. "There's a goddam snake right there!" he screamed. Then he paused, as though waiting for me to do something. Then he screamed again, "He's right there! Right there!"

"Well, shoot him," I said. "You've got the gun." I started walking toward him. He neither spoke nor moved. "Load the gun," I said, "and toss it to me when I get there. If it's that moccasin, you're not gonna scare him while he's in the water." Any pistol is hard to shoot if you're not experienced. With that thing of Arnold's, it would be nearly impossible. The best I hoped for was to hit close enough to jar it and make it move. But I looked at Arnold, furiously trying to load the gun, and grinned. "Somebody's gonna have to hit it."

He tossed me the gun. "Oh-my-God! Oh-my-God! Just let me get out of here. Just let me get out of this place."

"Or you could just walk around it," I said, "and come in up here."

"I don't want to move," he said. "It might strike."

"Suit yourself," I said, picking my way carefully down the steep vine-covered bank. "You see, a moccasin has a very special psychology. Its idea of pride is not to allow a human being to affect it in any way that it can possibly help. Hence, unlike most snakes, a moccasin is considerably less afraid of you than you are of it. Why I've seen moccasins latch onto fish that were on stringers, and guys would pick them up and haul them into the boat without even knowing they were on there, and the moccasin wouldn't even let go of the fish."

I could see the snake now, coiled in a lazy S in the water around the trunk of the little cypress where it had been perched earlier. "Arnold," I said, "I'm sure you could just walk around there and

49

come on in. You just have to understand the psychology of snakes, that's all."

"I do not want to move," he screamed, as though the snake were deaf. "I just don't want to move!" I didn't know—Were snakes deaf?

I finally got down as close as I wanted to, then stepped off to the side a way so that I could shoot away from Arnold. The snake still had not moved. I could see it clearly now, just below me on the bank. It was not a big one, but its coils were slow and thick and cold. Its black snout was just above the water, and the rest was just below.

The last few feet were slow. I extended the muzzle as close as I could to the moccasin's head, then settled against the bank and took aim. It was an experience, being this close to the thing and about to pull the trigger. I took an instant longer and let it sink in. Then I held my breath and began squeezing.

The sound of the shot surprised both Arnold and me; the impact seemed terribly close. Arnold bolted immediately for the shore and was standing beside me before I got the water wiped out of my eyes. At first all we could see was mud, where the snake had been. But then we saw the heavy black coils writhing and twisting over on themselves.

"It's not dead!" Arnold screamed. I didn't think I'd hit it, but it was plenty stunned. Arnold grabbed the pistol out of my hand as though I'd betrayed him, and he started blasting away again in the general direction of the water.

"Oh, my foot!" I screamed.

He looked at me.

"Don't worry. You didn't shoot it, but you might have. Now would you please cut that racket out? My ears are gone completely."

As is the case with most people who are afraid of many things, not the least of which is the fear of appearing cowardly, Arnold could get over a scare very quickly. He converted this one into rage. Never had he seen a more loathsome, despicable place than Mississippi. It was worse than when he had been in school here. While most of the nation had enjoyed unlimited progress, it had slipped backward into prehistory. Did I realize that it had about the lowest per-capita income in the nation? How I had stood being stuck here for all these years was more than he could imagine. I asked him if he hadn't forgotten something, indicating the log he had dropped. He condemned it obscenely, and we repaired to the fire for some lunch.

Arnold became suddenly loquacious.

Of the wine he had brought: "Now Chablis is very similar in bouquet to Liebfraumilch Glockenspiel if perhaps a shade heavier. However, I believe that you will find this quite satisfactory. I got it from a good friend of my father's down in New Orleans. He samples a bottle of every case that he sells, and he saves me what he considers the best. Now what I want him to get me is some good absinthe. . . ."

Or of the tobacco: "I noticed that you sampled some of this latakia. How did you like it?" I had found it quite satisfactory. "Actually it's a bit strong for the fireside, and I had saved it for our trip. I thought it would be better in a more robust atmosphere."

He was starting in on fishing tackle, but that led him to note that he had not had the opportunity to use the surf rod he had bought for this trip, which led him once again to the brink of commenting on our plight, which he now seemed to want to avoid. By then the steaks were ready. We were starving, and we ate in silence.

It was when I turned to reach for the wine bottle that I saw her.

"Arnold," I said softly, indicating with a nod, "we're not alone."

"Well I'll be damned," he said; and there was a long instant when the three of us stared in silence.

She was standing above us on the next higher bluff in what appeared to be the remnants of a formal ball gown, though it was so mud-stained and vine-ripped that it was hard to be sure. She had the ageless face of a beautiful idiot. Time had taken its toll, but not in the usual lines and creases of worry and dissipation. In her right hand she held a banjo, and her left covered her mouth with what in different circumstances would have been a theatrical gesture. As we stared at her, she also stared, but her gaze seemed directed rather at something on the ground. Finally I broke the trance by looking down for what might have her attention.

"Would you care to come up to the fire?" Arnold said, suddenly making an urgent effort to brush the mud from his clothes.

All I could see was Arnold's forgotten pistol. When I looked back, she was looking questioningly at me.

"Come ahead," I said. "We were just finishing lunch."

Then she came without speaking, walking despite all, like someone who had been to a charm school. Arnold jumped up, slapping wildly at the mud. "Have a seat, have a seat," he said. "Would you care for a steak? We've got plenty. How about some wine?"

"No," she said, glancing downward. She sat gracefully, so that you couldn't tell how she had arranged her legs under the long dress. I let Arnold take over.

"Well"—he laughed nervously—"Ah, we were on our way to— ah—the Chandeleur Islands for some fishing, and we were forced down by the storm last night." Her eyes proclaimed noncomprehension. "Ah—could you tell us by any chance where we are? You know, I mean, where the nearest town is?"

"Graceville?" she said questioningly, pointing back into the woods.

"Oh," Arnold said, nodding. "And that's where you're from? Graceville?"

She nodded.

"Well"—Arnold laughed out loud, fidgeting with his filthy pants —"I wonder if you could take us to—uh, a telephone or, or an airport or something. Someone who might help us with this airplane."

She didn't reply. She was looking intently at the pistol now, and fascination tinged with sadness filled her face. Arnold was flustered. She extended her hand for the gun but halted, hesitated, then withdrew. Hers no longer seemed the face of an idiot, but of a person obsessed. What had appeared at first as agelessness was dark, classical beauty, the rarest type which is neither prettiness nor cuteness nor—least of all—freshness. I sensed Arnold's disturbance and felt the need of rescuing him, but I could think of nothing to say or do. "Well"—I laughed myself—"isn't that something? And you say there's a town called Graceville not too far through the woods?"

All the while she had been staring at the gun, and I could tell immediately that what I had said hadn't helped. She shot me one glance, then looked at nothing. But Arnold seemed to take courage

52

from my failure. "You like the gun?" he said as though he were offering beads to a savage.

She trained her dark eyes on his face and left them there. "Yes," she said as frankly as anything I had ever heard.

I gave up completely and retired to watch.

"Here," he said, picking it up. "You can see it. You can have it if you promise not to shoot it." She took it. "Here," Arnold said, "let me get something out of it." But she snatched it away, and Arnold let her.

Then there was something else crashing through the brush. The woman let out a low cry. A huge bear of a man dressed in blue jeans and a checkered shirt burst out of the woods, saw us, and came limping toward the camp. "Anna," he said, staring from Arnold to me and back to Arnold, "you get back here!"

He was even bigger than Arnold, with powerful open hands the size of pie plates and thick as Bibles. But whereas Arnold was handsome, this man was hideously ugly. His head was a massive block implanted, with no neck, on shoulders that might have pushed boxcars. His legs were equally huge, but his right knee was stiff, resulting in the limp which made his walking noisy despite its speed which seemed to stem solely from a disregard for all impediments.

"Anna!"—he was on top of us—"Get back here."

She seemed about to bolt when he reached out and grabbed her arm.

"Let go of her." Arnold was on his feet. The man hoisted her to her own. "Get your goddam hands off." Arnold grabbed the man's wrist.

The next thing I saw, the man's fist was up in Arnold's throat, and Arnold was staggering backward. From the sound of the blow, it would have killed me, but Arnold was back on him as he was wrenching the gun from the girl's hand. "That's my gun," Arnold said, reaching once more for the hand that held the girl, but the man shoved him back and trained the muzzle on Arnold's chest. Arnold halted.

"Not anymore, it's not."

Arnold stood rocking, arrested, impotent, the rage flooding his cheeks.

"What chu-all doin' here with her?"

"Nothing," I said. "We were flying over last night in that airplane, and we got forced down by the storm. She just wandered up."

The man stood still for an instant, calculating.

The girl stared at the gun pointed at Arnold's chest.

"You're under arrest," he said. He needed a shave.

Arnold stared daggers at me.

"Who are you?" I said.

"I'm the Graceville town marshal." He offered no badge.

"What are we doing?" I asked.

"Faw the moment"—he took out a handkerchief and touched a bleeding briar scratch—"you trespassin' on the propity of Robe't V. Collins."

I looked at Arnold. There was an air of finality in the way the man had said it, as though by taking out the handkerchief he had dismissed anything further we might say. I couldn't think of what to do. He had the hammer back on Arnold's gun. When he put the handkerchief back, he looked at me again. "Let's go."

"What about the stuff?" I said.

"We'll send the niggras to get it." He motioned us out in front of him with the gun, and we started into the woods. After a little way a path materialized, and we followed it, like a tunnel through the all but solid vegetation. Arnold walked as though he were entranced. I began to sweat, and the mosquitoes swarmed about my head. I didn't look back at the man and the girl, but I could hear her tiny step-step-step, and his mighty step-slide, step-slide, and his heavy bestial breathing.

After a while I said without turning around, "Just who is this girl, anyway?"

"She's Robe't V. Collins's wife," he said.

"And what's she doing out here?"

"He's gone huntin'. She hea'd you-all shootin' and thought it was him, so she run off."

We walked long into the afternoon. Rain had transformed the path into a gully where we slipped and slid, soaking our clothes with the thick muddy water.

Arnold seemed stupefied, his strides long and automatic, his arms hanging limply at his sides, his jaw slack and immobile, and his eyes fixed on some nonexistent something slightly above the path. The girl, her legs hidden beneath the leaf-matted skirt, seemed to move among the puddles and downed branches with the combined agility and stately grace of a wise and beautiful doe, one who although temporarily caught and thwarted would escape again and again. After what? And the man, the beast of the heavy breathing, the stiff-legged beast, moved with the weight and quietude of inevitability, not around the vines and puddles, but through them, not because of anything, but despite everything, despite our hatred, despite his stiff leg, despite the ugliness. I moved neither despite nor because of anything. I moved with my feet which were walking, as though I were in a giant green intestine borne along in the peristaltic motion of the wind in the tunnel wall. To where? To what? To Graceville.

And then:

It wasn't a sound, but the sudden cessation of sound. I turned, and Arnold was still in the air, at the pause in mid-leap above the man like a savage in a war dance. The girl screamed, and I dove as the pistol came up. But it never went off. Arnold fell on the man, and the man didn't go down, didn't even look surprised. Arnold got his knees around the man's waist, with one hand on the wrist that held the gun and his other hand at the man's throat. Their faces were bare inches apart. "Pig shit!" Arnold said, and he spat in the man's face.

The man was slow, almost unimpressed. He stood there, looking at Arnold, supporting Arnold's weight, with Arnold's hand at his throat and Arnold's face proclaiming the strain in his every muscle. At one point Arnold's peace symbol brushed against his lips, and he spat it away.

"Filthy, slimy bigot," Arnold said. "I hate you. Do you know that? I hate you, and I'm going to kill you."

The man was still unimpressed. He watched Arnold for another moment, then raised the hand that Arnold seemed somehow to have ignored. He positioned the palm beside Arnold's head, then hit Arnold with it, hit him or shoved him or somehow propelled him backward along the same path he must have taken when he leapt.

55

Except that this time Arnold landed on his face. He didn't move. If I hadn't seen him breathing, I'd have thought him dead.

But for a third time the man was unimpressed. He picked Arnold up, turned him around, and set him on his feet. For a moment Arnold held the position in which the man placed him as though he were cast in iron. The blow had put his eyes out of focus, and his face was bruised and blackening. A subarticulate groan escaped him, and he made as if to take a step in no direction, then seemed to give it up and fall back tottering into the original pose in which the man had set him down.

"Get up," the man said to me.

I got up.

"Walk."

I walked. A second later I heard Arnold stumbling into motion behind me.

Twice inside the next quarter mile Arnold seemed to lose his direction and stagger off into the vines. Once the man steered him back into the trail. Later I disentangled him from a blackberry bush and helped him along for a few feet. No one spoke.

By the time we came in sight of a clearing, he seemed to be able to walk and hold a direction on his own.

Graceville wasn't much of a town. We came out of the woods at the low end of a dirt road on which were the prints of a few bare feet, an occasional boot, and some horseshoes. There were a few buildings along the road—a couple of houses, a couple of shacks, and something that might once have been a store or a warehouse which now looked completely disused. The buildings seemed incredibly old, all made of logs with cypress-shingled roofs, not run down in the sense of being about to cave in, but rather worn down as though time and weather had stripped them to the essence of their strength and durability. There were no signs of wires, no signs of lights, telephones, or plumbing. I could see a few Negroes milling around below us, past the end of the street. Beyond that was some water. I assumed—correctly as I later learned—that it was the river.

Arnold moved along the road as though in a trance. His eyes were uncrossed, and he was walking straight, but he didn't seem to notice that we had come out of the woods. His face was grotesquely swollen and about the color of a badly bruised plum. There was a big knot above one ear. But he didn't walk like someone who had just taken what he had. His eyes were open, and his mouth beneath the bruises was working almost as if he were lost in thought and talking to himself.

The man conducted us to a building which was, if anything, harder and more rugged-looking than the rest but lower, squatter, almost black. He motioned us inside without speaking.

There was only one room, but it was divided near the back by a crosshatching of iron bars set in the logs; the front part had a desk and some chairs; the back was totally unfurnished—a jail. I was going to ask what a place this small needed with a jail when I remembered a sentence spoken when I was a kid by some relative who was himself a small-town cop: "When you got niggers, you gotta have a jail." At the time I had accepted it as axiomatic, like "God made the world and all the children" or "Santa Claus has eight reindeer," and right then was the first time I got really scared, to have the man usher me through the tiny doorframe which seemed intended to accept horizontal rather than vertical forms, into this jail that I had the sudden feeling had no more business being here than the man in the moon.

I watched intently as he shoved Arnold's head down and under the doorframe with his practiced hands that commanded all at once the girl, Arnold, and the pistol that he had still not uncocked. The lock, at least, was citified. I would have expected something like in a Western, but it was a Slage and well oiled, and the man's hands manipulated the key with practiced efficiency. Then he took the girl's sleeve, and they left, and as he closed the door, the room became totally dark and the sound was flat and dry and wooden.

There was nothing to sit on, so I remained standing. Neither of us spoke. I couldn't see Arnold because there was not enough light, but I could tell where he was. He gave off a kind of heat or a vibration or something—I knew where he was! I stayed back and away. Then when my nose cleared from the walking, I began to smell the place; it grew and crept in to me out of the darkness, a fetid effusion of ammoniac shit reek like a bus-station bathroom. Slowly, very slowly, my eyes achieved some small adjustment to the darkness, and I could pick out Arnold's outline.

57

"Well," I said tentatively. "What do you think?"

"Think?" The shadow of his head shook from side to side as he slowly collapsed to the floor. "What's to think?"

I moved a step away from him and squatted, reluctant to sit on the floor for fear it might be the source of the smell.

"I guess you're right," I offered. "How's your face?"

"What?"

"Your face."

"Oh, it's all right. It's just fine."

"Well, good."

He shook his head.

I scratched a mosquito bite, and kind of leaned back against the wall.

"There's one thing for sure though," Arnold said.

"What's that?"

"That certainly was a beautiful woman to be in a place like this."

"Little bit crazy though, I'd say."

"You might be too, if you'd been through what she has," Arnold retorted.

"What's that?"

"They torture her here," Arnold said.

"What?"

"They do!" He turned excitedly to me, "You can tell it. I've had cases like that. S. and M. cases. The eyes! Did you see the eyes, Fargus? And the fascination with the gun. It's a textbook case."

"Whatever you say," I said.

Arnold froze in the position of his talking. There was another long silence. Who could tell how long in a place where nothing moved, where there was no light?

"What's going to happen to us, Fargus?"

"It's an interesting question."

"God, she was beautiful."

"What's that got to do with it?"

"Nothing. Maybe everything."

"What?"

"You mean you couldn't tell it, Hank? Couldn't see it on her? Almost smell it!"

"No. No! What the hell are you talking about?"

"Fargus?"

"What?"

"This isn't—" he hissed. "This isn't just like an ordinary island. Things go on here. . . . There's a different law here. It's another world!"

I looked away from him and rubbed my eyes. Then I rubbed my neck. Then I looked back at him. "Well, I will tell you one thing," I said. "If I know anything at all about this sort of people, the first thing they're gonna think is that we were messing around with your woman, there. And if I were you, I wouldn't say or do anything that'd give them any excuse at all for thinking it."

"Do you suppose they'll try us?" he shot.

"How could they? Do you think there's a judge in this town?"

"We have the right to make a phone call," he said.

"There isn't any phone, Arnold."

"That doesn't matter," he insisted. "We have a right!"

"You bet," I said. "You just bet we do."

There was another long silence.

"Fargus," he said. "When we get out of here, we're gonna take that woman with us."

"Right," I said. "And when is that gonna be?"

"I don't know. We'll break out and steal a car. We'll get back and call my lawyer. She doesn't deserve this—not that beautiful woman."

"Arnold," I said, "there aren't any cars. This is an island. Right down there at the end of the street is the Mississippi River. It goes clear around half the island, and the lake goes around the rest. There's nothing where they join but swamp. There's not but one road on the whole island, and that's right outside the door. It's not a hundred yards long."

He said nothing. These were insignificant details. His face was turned up. He was seeing something in the darkness.

All of a sudden I squared around and faced him. "Arnold," I said, "goddamm it, where's your head? Now listen—listen! We may be in one helluva mess—"

"Fargus," he said very quietly.

59

"What?"

"I can't get that woman off my mind."

I stared at his black outline. "Lord have mercy," I said. I turned back around and leaned against the wall.

Then the door opened, and a sudden glare burst upon the room. A gaunt, aged, tonsured Negro entered, looked at us, and said, "I'm sorry."

Arnold and I looked at each other, then back at the Negro. He had three blankets in one hand and a smoking pot in the other, and he was having trouble with the door. Arnold and I stood up. When he got inside, he set the blankets on the table and the pot on the floor. He thrust a long, black, incredibly thin arm deep into one of his pockets and seemed to search for something. "I'm sorry," he said before he found it.

"That's all right," Arnold said.

The Negro ignored Arnold. Finally, he produced a long sulphur match which he began striking against the table top. The match broke, and he said, "I'm sorry." He picked up the part with the head on it and struck it again. This time it ignited with a flare and reek that cut through the darkness and the smell of the cell. Then he began trying to remove the chimney from a small coal-oil lamp on the table. The match was nearly out before he touched it to the wick, but it caught, and again he said, "I'm sorry," as the room filled with light.

He turned and picked up the blankets and the pot. For an instant he seemed puzzled about what to do with them. Finally he put the whole works down, took one of the blankets, and set it aside, then brought the others over to the bars. There was one spot where the bars were bent out slightly and the sides of the pot were bent in, so that it just fit. The Negro passed it through the opening and waited while Arnold took it by the handle. Then he started stuffing the blankets through the same hole, saying "I'm sorry, I'm sorry" all the time.

"It's all right," Arnold said, as though he were talking to a patient or a child. "It's perfectly all right."

The Negro ignored him. The pot had slipped perfectly through the bent bars and would have fit nowhere else; he made his bed expertly on an old mattress behind the desk. It was only in between tasks that he seemed confused.

"Now don't you worry about a thing," Arnold was telling him as the Negro apologized for handing us some spoons. "It's all going to be all right. Now you just sit down, and we'll get it all straightened out. Okay?"

Finally the Negro stopped and stared at Arnold, rubbing the back of his bent spindly neck. "Whuz da matta?" he said. "You goan ca'plain bout yo' stew? Ah sweah ta goo'ness, you jailbuds is all alike." Then he sat down at the desk by the lamp, took a bottle of Bengué Liniment out of one of the desk drawers, and began massaging his neck and back, rocking back and forth, chanting, "I'm sorry. Oh, Lawd Jesus, I'm sorry."

Arnold met my eyes. Arnold touched his temple with his index finger and nodded knowingly at me. I nodded back, then sat down on the blanket and looked at the stew. There were no plates, only the spoons and the pot, but despite everything, the food smelled good. It contained plenty of meat. I tried a spoonful. "Not bad," I said to Arnold. The meat tasted like venison. He was scraping the bottom of the pot before we set it aside.

I dragged my blanket over to the wall, rolled it into a cushion, and relaxed against it. The combination of the lamp and the liniment had destroyed the bad smell. I belched and wished I had something to smoke. Arnold was staring at the Negro. "Uh, excuse me," I said. "Mister, sir."

The old man turned, looking annoyed, and said, "I'm sorry."

"It's all right," I said. "You don't suppose there's any way I could get something to smoke?"

"I'm sorry," he said and began rummaging in the same drawer that had held the liniment.

"Think nothing of it," I said, winking at Arnold.

Finally he produced a bent Prince Albert can and a sheaf of stained cigarette papers. He poked them through the bars, and I took them, nodding. He never stopped massaging his neck, but he fixed my gaze once before he sat back down. "You jailbuds is all alike," he said.

I had never rolled a cigarette, but Arnold could do it well. He

61

made us each one, and we sat back smoking and staring once again at the Negro.

"Uh, thank you very much for the tobacco," Arnold said.

"I'm sorry," the Negro said.

"That's all right," Arnold said. "Uh, could you tell me who that girl is—the one that was with that big man when they brought us in?"

"She'll be here," the Negro said.

"When?" Arnold said.

"Da night befo' da hangin'," the Negro said. "I'm sorry. Oh, Lawd Jesus, I'm sorry."

"Oh," Arnold said. "I see." He leaned back, looking at me, exhaling thin pencils of smoke from his nostrils.

I shook my head.

Arnold looked back at the Negro, staring for several minutes until he finished the cigarette. Then he began, slowly, carefully, rolling another. "You say," he said, "she'll be here—the night before the hanging?"

"I'm sorry," the Negro said.

"How do you know she'll be here?"

"She always be here," he said, moaning and rocking with his massage. "Evah night befo' th' hangin', she run off an' be wif da man dey gonna hang."

I saw Arnold's lips form into a sudden "Oh," but the word went unsaid. His eyes were wide, as though he had made some great secret discovery, and he looked across at me and then back, rocking along with the Negro.

"And just"—Arnold glanced at me, then back at the Negro as though this were the clincher—"who is it they're gonna hang?"

The Negro looked directly at him, terribly annoyed. "W'y you!" he said. "Jest soon as Mist Collins git back." Then as though dismissing the whole matter: "All you jailbuds jest zackly alike."

Arnold watched him intently, silently, until his rocking became rhythmic, until he seemed oblivious to everything except his own apologies and the sensations in his back. Then as quick and silent as a cat Arnold was beside me.

"I can see it," he said, "I can see it exactly now."

"Well, I'm glad of that," I whispered.

"We wait until that night when she comes, and then we make our break."

"And how do you suggest we manage it? Are you going to break down the bars and repair the airplane right on the spot?"

"It'll be risky," he said, "very risky. But I think we can do it. Just let me think."

"All right," I said, "you think about it, hear? But promise me one thing. Promise me you won't do anything crazy until she comes. Okay?"

"Sure. Sure," he said. "That's all part of it. Now just let me think."

"Okay," I said. "I'm tired. I'm going to sleep."

When I closed my eyes, Arnold was in his corner, intently rolling another cigarette.

What did I think? Nothing at all. I heard. I saw. I thought nothing.

Until, "Fargus!"

"What—?" I woke with a start, not knowing where I was. Weathermore was in my face, shaking me, his teeth white in the dark. "Jesus! What is it?"

"Fargus, I had a dream!"

"A dream?"

"A nightmare!"

"Oh, my God!" I sat up, rubbing my face, trying to get some kind of bearing in the darkness. I grabbed Arnold's hand to make him quit shaking me, and he grabbed mine back and held it, but at least the shaking had stopped. "Take it easy. Take it easy, okay? What time is it?"

"I don't know what time it is. Oh, God, Fargus, you wouldn't believe the dream I just had."

"Okay. It's all right. Calm down. What? What was it?"

"They were killing a black."

"Uh-huh?"

"They were hanging him and shooting him and burning him."

"Right," I said. "Right. So what happened?"

"It was me!"

3

"Kwhump!" Something hit the side of the building, waking me from a surprisingly deep sleep. *"Gawaaak, whap whap whap, gawaaak! gawaak!"*

The windowless jail was very dark, but I could see a brilliant gleam coming through a chink in the east wall. Arnold and the Negro were asleep. I crawled over to the chink and put my eye to it. It was about an inch by a half inch in size, and as soon as my eye adjusted to the glare, I had an adequate view of what was happening.

At first, all I could see was the rooster, a big, vicious-looking Rhode Island red, hackles flared, wings up, beak open, not a yard from the chink. Its spurs were the size of pencils.

Then an axe sang past its head, barely missing, and the chicken ran squawking across the bare earth and came to bay under a tree. Now I could see the enemy—the stiff-legged man of the day before —appearing from the left, his backside broad and brown stained. He was caressing the axe, walking slowly toward the chicken and speaking gently to it.

"Yes," said the man.

"Awk," said the chicken.

"I could tell from Laurie's eggs."

"Awk?"

"I could tell from Laurie's eggs. Uh-huh. You been gettin' just a little too much nookie for your own good."

"Awk-awk." The chicken shook its head.

"And now you gonna pay, chicken," said the man, walking slowly, speaking gently, caressing the blade.

"Awk!"

"Mist Ernest, she says, that big ole roost' jest rurnin' all them eggs. Uh-huh, and that means you."

"Awk!"

"And you gonna pay, chicken! You gonna be jailbird feed. You gonna pay. You gonna be executed with this here axe."

He was very close now, but the chicken stood its ground. There was no sound from either of them. The man slowly drew the axe over his shoulder. He poised, waiting, each intently watching the other. Then both moved. Feathers flew, and the man screamed, and blood gushed from the chicken's wing and went all over the man, and the man was trying to reach the ankle of his stiff leg where more blood was soaking his pants, and the chicken fled in a skewed circle. I began keeping a mental scoreboard: "Top of the second. Chicken, 1; Ernie, 1."

But Ernie began to break the rules. His spurred leg was bleeding badly, and he couldn't reach it. He went into a rage, charging the chicken which, though still able to run much faster than Ernie, seemed unable with its one and a half wings to control its direction. He hit it a vicious wallop with the flat of the axe, lofting the bird in a cloud of bloody feathers, but it landed running, and Ernie made three wild swipes through the air. Now both went wild. The chicken was everywhere, on top of Ernie, between his legs, covering him with bloody feathers, until finally out of the confusion came one bone-crushing thud, and the action ended.

I heard Arnold stirring in his blankets, but I didn't move. Ernie was covered with feathers. I could tell from the thickness of the blood on his foot that he was in trouble. He picked up the chicken and disappeared in the direction of the door. Then he burst inside, blinked at the darkness, and kicked viciously at the sleeping Negro.

"Sorry!" he bellowed. Arnold jumped upright. "You low-rate lazy black son of a bitch, get your ass out of the sack and take this here down to Laurie. Tell her here's her goddam chicken."

"I'm sorry! I'm sorry!" The blankets were squirming.

"Oh, God! My foot."

"I am a black," Arnold said.

"I'm sorry! I'm sorry! Oh, Lawd Jesus, I'm sorry."

"You lazy, low-rate—Oh, shit!"

Sorry was up. Ernie was down. The chicken was on the floor.

"I'm a black, and I'll thank you not to refer to persons of my race in that way," Arnold said.

"Oh, shit!" Ernie was rocking back and forth the way Sorry had done the night before. His entire foot was brilliant carmine. "Oh, shit. I b'lieve I'd rather get shot." The blood was thick and pasty— a very bad sign for him.

"I'm sorry."

"Goddam nigger."

"I am a black."

"Goddam you too, then."

"I'm sorry, I'm sorry." Picking up the bird and scurrying out the door.

Arnold shut up.

"Oh, Lord."

"Pardon me," I said, "but—"

"Fuck you, jailbud. Are you a nigger, too?"

"No," I said. "I'm a doctor."

"You kiddin'?"

"No, he is, too."

"But he's a nigger."

Arnold was haughtily silent.

"Right."

"Well, what's that got to do with anything? What do I care if the jailbuds is doctors or niggers or both?"

"This," I said. "If the right thing doesn't get done about your foot, you're gonna be dead inside two months."

"From a foot?"

"You ever hear of tetanus? Gangrene? You happen to remember what chickens walk around in all day?"

"What's that?"

"Chicken shit."

"Oh." He stared at the foot, trying to detect a piece.

"That's all right. You don't have to be able to see it. It's got germs, little bitty bugs so small you can't see them."

"I know about germs, for Chris' sake."

"Scuse me."

He was staring intently at the foot, touching it and wincing when he did.

"Hurts, doesn't it?"

"You goddam right. Look, jailbud, what are you gettin' at?"

"Not a damn thing, except if you don't let a doctor take care of that foot, you're gonna be dead inside of two months. Dead, Mr. Tough. Do you know what that is?"

He stared a long time, then looked up. "So what'm I s'posed to do? Let some half-assed nigger doctor go pokin' around with it?"

"Don't you call me nigger," I said.

Arnold jumped.

"Look, jailbud." He tried to rise, winced, and nearly fell before he could sit back down. "Okay. Okay." He spoke much more softly. "Just *zackly* what are you gettin' at?"

"Nothing. Not a damn thing. Just that me and this nigger here are the only doctors on this island, is all."

Arnold was staring at me as if he wanted my blood. I tried with quick glances and hand motions to calm him down and get him to understand that it was for both of us. He spread his lips and prissed at me, then began elaborately examining the log wall, trying to figure out what kind of tree it came from or something.

"Okay," Ernie said, taking Arnold's still cocked revolver out of the desk drawer and pointing it frankly at Arnold. "Big 'un, you stay rat where you at."

Arnold jumped, then ignored him even more intently by turning his attention to the ceiling.

"You gidover by the door," Ernie said to me.

In my own time I obeyed.

Then he unlocked the door. I paused on the threshold and grabbed Ernie's hand when he reached to drag me out. But I wasn't starting anything. I just held his hand off me and stepped out on my own. Arnold jumped again when Ernie slammed the door, but never once looked back around.

"You're gonna have to stay off that foot for several days," I said. "Where do you wanna stay?"

He looked at it, sulky like a hurt child. "At t' house, I reckon."

"Where is that?"

"Up the road."

"Well, I guess you could walk that far before I get it dressed. A little more right now isn't going to make that much difference."

Then he looked at me and there was something new in his face, something I'd have hardly thought it could have shown. "You could help me," he said.

"Yeah," I said. "I guess I could at that."

He waited a second longer, then with one hand still holding the pistol, laid the other arm across my shoulders, and with him limping magnificently and me staggering under half his weight, we headed for the outer door.

We made slow progress up the dirt street. He leaned heavily on my shoulder and before long my knees were threatening to buckle. I kept thinking that his foot really shouldn't be hurting him that badly. But he kept looking at my face, hawking my expression. "Hey," I said.

He stopped.

"Listen, man, I gotta rest a minute. You're about to shove me into the ground."

He tottered on one foot, then let himself down. He seemed to have forgotten the pistol.

"How," I said, "am I gonna get back to the jail when we get finished? You're not gonna be able to walk at all then, and I'm sure as hell not gonna carry you."

"Ole Beard be long. He carry you back."

"I see," I said. "And just who is Ole Beard?"

He looked down and shook his head, gave a mirthless chuckle. "You'll find out."

"Uh-huh. Well maybe you better tell me now. I may not want to go back with him."

"What the hell you thank you goan do 'bout it?"

"Oh, nothing! Not a thing! I just kinda like to know what I'm getting into is all." Then I added, "Before I go giving out free medical treatment, and all that." Ernie thought a second. "Ole Beard's a son of a bitch," he said.

"I see," I said.

"You'll find out," Ernie said. "Now let's go."

So we got up and went.

About halfway up the street, we came to two cabins. One was clean, neat, and in good repair, but Ernie gestured toward the other. The first, he said, belonged to Sorry and Laurie. Ernie lived alone; that much was apparent from the sight and smell of his house. Outside, the shingles were loose, and the roof of the porch was caving in. Inside, it was filthy. There was one room, containing a cot, a tin stove, and a three-legged table that held a huge, dusty Bible. Arnold's and my duffel bags were just inside the door.

I helped Ernie onto the cot, and he thanked me. Then I looked quickly around. Above the door, in ludicrous contrast to the rest of the house, hung a lavishly engraved, Purdy 10-gauge. I commented on it as he settled into the pillow.

"Mist Collins give it to me when my wife died," he said. "Take it down if you want to."

I did. "This is a helluva note," I said. "There you sit with a loaded pistol ready to blow the hell out of me if I try anything, and you invite me to look at this."

"Ain't no shells," he said. "Mist Collins keeps all them."

"Huh." I replaced the gun. "Look"—I took a bottle of whiskey out of one of the bags—"What I gotta do to your foot is liable to hurt like hell." I shook the bottle in front of his face. "Why don't you chug-a-lug about half what's left, and let it take effect real good before I start."

He almost reached for it, then stopped. His brows lowered. "Uh-uh. I ain't drankin' no whiskey while you settin' here outa jail. You leave that bottle right here on the floor, and if I need any, I'll drank it after you gone."

I set it down. He picked it up, looked at it with obvious pleasure, then set it back down. "Tough it out then," I said.

I got the first-aid kit out of my duffel bag and washed his foot, gently at first with only water. He was staring at me, perplexed. Then I got the 70 per cent rub. I glanced at him. He was staring at me. I soaked a cotton ball and pushed it against the raw flesh of his ankle. "Goddam son of a bitch!" he screamed, wild-eyed and waving the pistol in the air. But he never once pointed the pistol at me. You bastard, I thought. When I took the cotton away, he lay still, chewing on his lower lip. I bandaged him up.

"What now?" I said, replacing the kit.

"We wait."

"For what?" I stared directly at him.

"Somebody git in to take you back to jail," he said weakly, but he pointed the gun a little more in my direction.

"Well," I said, looking and then sitting down. "Do you mind if I get a pipe?"

"Git it," he said.

I began rummaging through the pack. He was watching me, but he didn't look suspicious. I shrugged, got the pipe out, loaded it, and lit up. It was good, the first one of the morning. I leaned against the pack and relaxed.

Ernie, looking at me, said nothing.

"So when are they gonna take me back to jail?"

"They be in aftah a while."

"Where are they now?"

"They run a trotline in the river. Got a big gill net, too."

"I see." I blew a smoke ring, and Ernie's eyes grew wide as he watched it rise and dissipate. "Is fish all y'all got to eat around here?"

"Naw." His eyes darted back to me. "Niggers got a garden back up yonder. Chickens. Usta have pigs and cows, but they all bust loose. Now the cows is all gone, and all the pigs we get is what we can shoot."

"I see," I said. I blew another smoke ring; this really amazed Ernie. "How many people live here?"

"Well, le's see." He looked back at my face. "They's me and Mist Collins and his wife. Then they's Ole Beard and Young Beard and Miz Beard. That's all the white. Then there's ten, 'leven, twelve, twelve niggers and Mist Collins' nigger and Sorry and Laurie."

"That's fifteen niggers and six white."

"Right," he said.

"How's your foot?" I asked.

"Feel's pretty good," he said.

I nodded. He nodded. Then I put down the pipe and looked at him seriously. "You say this Mr. Collins owns the whole island?"

"Yep."

"And just who is he? What does he do?"

"What do you mean, What does he do?"

"I mean what does he do with the island."

"Lives on it," Ernie said, disturbed.

"Of course," I said, and looked away.

"Well I mean—How the hell should I know? He stays gone all the time."

"Well, where does he go?" I shot back.

"Huntin'."

"I see. He keeps the whole island to hunt on?"

Ernie screwed up his forehead.

"Well, don't you even know him?"

"You goddam right I know him. I guess I ought to. We growed up together."

"Here?"

"Right here."

"Well, what does he do with the island then?"

"His old man owned the island before him, and his grandpappy before him, and I don't know no further back than that." Ernie was blushing.

"Here," I said, reaching quickly for the bottle, "are you sure you don't want a slug of this?"

He shook his head warily.

"Well, do you mind if I have one?"

He shook his head again. I held the bottle up and took a very light sip. When I set it down, he snatched it and took a long pull. I could tell by the bubbles.

"Good stuff," I said.

He nodded, eyes brimming.

"So Robert Collins got the island from his father."

"Yeah."

"And he hasn't ever done anything with it but hunt."

"Well, he usta be a preacha," Ernie said, as though it were something any fool should know.

"He's a preacher then," I said.

Ernie nodded.

"Who does he preach to around here?"

"Don't preach to nobody no more."

"But he's the same age as you."

"We growed up together," said Ernie, nodding. Then almost apologetically, "His maw wanted him to be a preacher. His ole man married her in New Orleans and brought her back here, but she hated it cause there wasn't nowhere to go to church. So she brung Mist Robert up to be a preacha."

"But his old man didn't want him to," I said.

"He didn say much about it, I reckon. Least not till his old lady died."

"What happened then?"

71

"His old man never said much about nothin'," Ernie said. "Still, he wadn' the kind you wanna mess around with." He picked up the whiskey, looked at it, then set the pistol down to unscrew the cap. I blew another smoke ring. "The night Mist Collins' old lady died, him and his old man had a helluva fight. Next mornin' Mist Collins was gone."

"Where to?"

Ernie shrugged. "Wherever you go to get to be a preacher," he said. "After that, his ole man just sort of shriveled up. Inside a year, he's dead. Well, purty soon Mist Collins shows up sayin' he's a preacha, and he's done prayed his ole man dead for his sins. He's got that crazy wife of his with him too. They moved into the big house and he starts preachin' to e'body in Graceville."

"What'd he preach about?"

Ernie looked puzzled. "How the hell should I know?"

"Well, didn't you listen?"

"E'body hop to and lissen. Scared he'd pray 'em dead if they don't."

"Hmm," I said. "And do you believe he prayed his old man dead?"

"Well, I ain't sayin' I don't nor I do. But seein' as I grew up with him and all, me and him been huntin' together since we's six, I do know he's the kind of fella if he want somebody dead, and he b'lieve the Lawd wants 'em dead, he'd see to it somehow that they died."

"I see," I said. "Just how many has he seen to like that?"

Ernie shrugged. "Bunch of niggers. Freddy Greenwell for sayin' he don't need nobody's preachin'. Couple more."

"Lord," I said. "What did he do to them?"

"Hung the white ones. He shot a couple of the niggers, I think."

"Doesn't he know that's against the law?"

"I'm the law," Ernie said, defensively. "He tells me who to get, and I put 'em in the jail."

"I mean outside law."

"Ain't never been no outside law in here," he said. "Fore you all came there ain't never been no outside nobody here."

"Never?"

"Not since the river changed course. That was in the twenties, in the big flood."

"I see," I said. "Well, what about that wife of his?"

"What about her?"

"What part does she take in the executions?"

"What do you mean?"

"Sorry said something. . . ."

"What he say?"

"Something about every night before they hang somebody, she comes and spends the night with them."

"I don't know nothin' about that," Ernie said. "I don't take no truck with Mister Collins' hangin'."

"You don't? I thought you were the law?"

"I just put 'em in the jail," he said dejectedly. "Hangin's between Ole Beard and Mist Collins."

"And his wife?"

"I don't know. I don't know nothin' bout that." He looked away and clammed up.

It was a long slow afternoon. A little old nigger woman who looked like a walking mummy came around about noon with a pot full of the offending chicken and some surprisingly good dumplings. We ate, and then Ernie drank some more of the whiskey, and after a while I looked up and noticed that he was sound asleep.

The thought crept in to me that if only I were quiet, I could get up and leave. I could even get the revolver; it had fallen from Ernie's hand onto the bed.

But what about Arnold?

This is what I could do: I could get the gun and slip out, go up to the jail, and spring Arnold—somehow. But where were the keys? What if I ran into somebody on the way? Well, I'd have the pistol —but would I use it? Should I use it? What if Robert Collins came after me? The idea of Robert Collins' coming after me kind of chased the rest of it out of my mind. I got up and walked over to the door, staring out into the quiet green afternoon.

There was nothing moving in Graceville, no human, no animal— no wind! I stood there staring for an unmeasured stretch, then sud-

73

denly had a maddening urge to move, do something, anything. I turned around and looked at Ernie. He hadn't moved. The gun was right there by his hand.

Then for some reason I started thinking about the stupid research. Stupid—that was what it seemed. What did the Fargus technique have to do with standing in the door of Ernie's house thinking about springing Arnold out of jail with a pistol and trying to escape in a broken airplane? Still it was there—like a big piece of one thing that wouldn't fit into a bigger piece of something else, so the two of them just rattled around in my head, giving me the urge to do something that another part of me was screaming I had no business doing.

For a bad second I had a feeling in me that bore an eerie resemblance to the look on Arnold's face. But no! No. I wasn't going to have that. The hell with it, all of it. It just wasn't time yet. I needed to know a lot more about the way this island worked before I even started thinking about it—about anything. The time would come. It would have to—but not yet.

I turned away from the door and walked noisily back across to where Ernie was lying on the cot. The gun was still there. I didn't touch it.

But I was still looking at it when the hand grabbed me on the shoulder, and I was in the air when I realized that I hadn't even heard anyone come into the room, and when I hit the floor, I saw him.

His head was tiny, shaven; the skin sucked up around the bones and muscles and dried there, hard and smooth and completely without expression. His eyes were as flat and shallow a blue as if they had been painted on. His beard from which, I suppose, he took his name was more like a wisp of Spanish moss that he held clamped in his mouth. It took me a second—then, "Ernie!" I yelled. And couldn't think of anything else to say.

But Ole Beard had turned away from me. He was staring at Ernie now.

Ernie was blinking himself awake.

Ole Beard stared at him until he sat up, and their eyes met, but Ernie's immediately cringed away.

Ole Beard did not move his eyes.

Ernie tried to look back up, but when he caught Beard's gaze, he cringed again.

Then Ole Beard snatched the revolver, and Ernie jerked his hand away. Ole Beard spat on Ernie's bed. "Asleep," he said, holding the gun by the cylinder. Then he turned on me.

He didn't tell me to get up; he kicked me in the ribs. I got up.

He gestured once, and I started walking. I couldn't hear him walking behind me. Outside the house I turned, and he was there, not a foot away with the gun in my face. "Wait a minute, goddamm it," I said. "What do you think you're doing?"

He had let the hammer down. Now he pulled it back.

I stared a second longer, then turned and resumed walking.

We walked a little farther; then all of a sudden I turned around again, and this time I didn't even know what I'd turned around for, but I did know that I didn't care whether he shoved the gun in my face or not, because I wasn't going to turn back and do what he said until something happened. "God damn you," I said. "What is going on here?"

But this time he didn't raise the gun. He just stood there. After a second the crack inside his beard opened, and there escaped what I suppose passed in him for a laugh. "Gud ain't dimnin' me," he croaked. "It's you He's dimnin'. You an' at t'ere spotted ape you brung wi' ye."

"What are you talking about?" I said.

He almost looked away, almost took his eyes off me, but not quite. "Shet up," he said, "an' git movin'."

After a second I turned and walked very slowly back to the jail.

Arnold was sitting in the corner when we came in. He jumped when we opened the door, and as soon as he saw who it was, he resumed his sulking. I cursed him under my breath. For some reason, I had found myself halfway hoping he would be enough crazier than me to start something and that between us we'd be able to give this Beard what I felt he needed. But Arnold only stared at the wall while Ole Beard let me back in the cell. He didn't move again until Ole Beard was gone.

Then he sat up as I sat down. We looked at each other, then away. Arnold began rolling a cigarette. He finished it and lit up.

"Can I have one?" I said softly.

He gave me his hurt-puppy look, as though I had betrayed him by being gone all day and that I now had a lot of nerve to ask for anything.

I looked away in disgust. For some reason the room was hot. The air was close and sultry.

"What's been going on?" he said. He watched my face for the disgust to leave.

"Well," I said, "I learned something about the predicament we're in."

"Good." He began rolling my cigarette. "I hoped you might," he added.

He rolled the cigarette very carefully and intently. Then he handed it to me with pride and lit it for me. "Thank you," I said.

"What are they gonna do to us?" he said.

I laughed nervously. "I was too scared to ask that."

He laughed too, and then we laughed together.

"Well what did you find out?" he asked.

So while we smoked, I told him about Ernie and what he had said about the island and about Robert Collins. He listened with a sort of strange detachment, seeming to pay more attention to the cigarette than to my words.

When I finished, he said, "So it seems like the only way out would be the airplane."

"Huh," I said. Then, "Oh, sure."

He snickered and shook his head as though he had been listening to the plottings of a child.

"I don't know," I said. "I told Ernie he'd have to stay off his feet and I'd have to come change his bandage every day, so I'll keep my ears open."

Arnold stared at me again as though I'd wounded him, then snickered again, shaking his head. "These rednecks are all alike," he said, "all religious fanatics."

I looked away and crushed out my cigarette. We fell into silence.

The day had tired me thoroughly, much more than had the physical exercise of the day before. The air was fetid and breathless. I bet that it was fixing to rain outside. My legs were jumpy, and my thoughts were racing. I dreaded trying to sleep.

Then I caught a movement and looked up. Arnold saw it too.

76

The door to the building had opened, and in the half light, etched against the sky, stood the woman, Anna, her hand over her mouth in the same theatrical gesture as the day before, wearing the same dress, staring the same fascinated stare—at us, at Arnold or me, or both. Nothing happened for a period as timeless as her face was ageless. Then Arnold tried to speak, but the sound died in his throat. The woman didn't move. Neither did I. And then the door closed, and she was gone.

Arnold and I slowly looked at each other. Sorry had never stirred. I pointed nervously toward the cigarette makings. Arnold glanced at them and back at me. Then nerves forced him to move, and he began working with shaking fingers.

"What does she want?" I whispered.

Arnold stared at me in disbelief.

"Hurry up with the cigarettes," I said.

"We're never gonna get outa here," Arnold said. "At least I'm not."

"Why you?" I said.

"Because I'm a nigger, and they're gonna lynch me," he said. "And because of her."

"What do you mean, Because of her?" I said. "You mean because you tried to keep Ernie off of her?"

He left my question hanging until he finished the cigarettes and we had them lighted.

Then he said, "Because it was me she was looking at. And because I wanted her to look at me."

I took a drag off my cigarette so vicious that it nearly disintegrated in my mouth. Then I stomped it on the floor and turned on Arnold.

But he beat me. "Let 'em," he hissed. "Just let 'em. But by God I'll have her first, and by God I'll take some of 'em with me when they do."

"Arnold, wait a minute!"

He was silent.

"What is this thing with you and her?"

"It's purity, Fargus."

"Purity?"

"It's I don't give a shit anymore, Fargus. It's real. It's real be-

77

cause when we're dead, we're gonna be really dead, and when I have her, that's gonna be just as real as death."

"What makes you think you're gonna have her? Not that stupid nigger—"

"I know it, Fargus."

"How, Arnold?"

He stared at me, less like he was thinking than like he was coming to a head inside. Then he went off:

"Do you remember what we did the night my father died?"

"We went to a nigger whorehouse so you could get laid."

"That was real, Fargus. And I knew it was coming. I knew the night we spent in that nigger hotel that it was coming. I could tell the death was in him. Nigger death. And that's what it smells like—a nigger whorehouse. And that's how this place smells. And that's how that girl smells—only purer."

"Purer?"

"More absolute."

"Jesus, Arnold," I rubbed my eyes with my hands and shook my head.

And that must have made him mad because he piled viciously into his blankets and covered his face and did not move.

I watched him a second, then turned my head, sitting on, staring into the darkness. Sometime later I must have gone to sleep, because I remember thinking I saw the door open again, but this time instead of the woman it was Ole Beard that stuck his face in the door, and it was like I was getting up and banging on the bars, trying to get out because I wanted to get at him and try to kill him, but I couldn't get out and he just stood there laughing at me.

And then sometime after that, the door did open, and it really was him. But instead of being light outside, it was still dark, and I had a hard time getting waked up and separating what was really going on from what I'd dreamed. Instead of laughing, Ole Beard came over and unlocked the cell, dragged me out, and shoved me toward the door. I was too close to sleep to say or do anything. When we stepped outside into the gray dawn, he pointed me in the direction of Ernie's house.

I walked to Ernie's house without protesting, just trying to keep a bearing on where I was, just trying to get waked up. When we got up onto Ernie's porch, he shoved me inside the door, then spun on his heel, and left me there.

"It's mighty early in the morning," I said to Ernie as Ole Beard disappeared wordlessly into the dawn. "What's the matter, your foot worse? Ole Motormouth there wouldn't tell me a thing."

He was looking up, bright-eyed from the bed, and when I said Motormouth, he chuckled. "What's matter"—he looked down again—"you don't like it?"

"Well, I was asleep."

"Well, screw you then, jailbud. Only time it was anybody to bring you."

"Okay. Okay. How is your foot?"

"Don't hurt."

"Well, good. Lemme look at it."

He swung around on the bed and stuck it out in front of him. I knelt down and began unwinding the bandage. He could have walked on it, but I wasn't about to tell him so. I squeezed hard, and he winced satisfactorily, but there was no pus, no sign of infection, just good clean blood which I held up on the gauze pad for him to see. "You're healthy as a bull," I said. "No reason why you shouldn't be up and around in about a week."

He grunted.

I replaced the bandage and sat down across from him in the only chair. "Well, what now? We just sit here all day?"

"What's matter? You don't like that?"

"I didn't say that. I just wondered what we're gonna do."

"We gonna sit here."

"Oh," I said. "I see."

He said nothing. His pupils were dilated. I glanced about for the whiskey bottle and found it just about empty under the edge of the bed.

I said nothing, and neither did he.

"So we're just gonna sit here all day," I said.

"Laurie bring breakfast in a minute."

"Good," I said.

He nodded with a trace of a smile. I nodded.

Frowning, Ernie was ugly, but there was a certain esthetic unity about him. Smiling, he was hideous. "You like scrammeled aigs 'n lean bacon?"

"Sure do."

"Better'n you'd get at the jail."

"I can imagine."

"Ain't you glad to be out for the day?"

"Well, sure. I mean . . . ."

"Well, just t'hell with it then."

"What? What's wrong? No kidding?"

"No shit?"

"No shit."

"Aw, I dunno. I mean, yesterday we had such a good talk."

"Oh," I said. "Sure. Sure."

He looked at me smiling. I smiled back.

"Laurie be here in a minute with breakfast."

"Great," I said. "I'm starving."

He sat back, smiling. I smiled back.

In a minute Laurie was there with breakfast. We ate in silence. It was delicious.

When we finished, he looked up and smiled. I smiled back.

"How do you like your steaks?" he said.

"What do you mean?" I said.

"Venison," he said. "We gonna have venison steaks for lunch."

"Great," I said. "Uh, medium."

"Laurie!" he bawled.

We waited the minute it took her to get there.

"Laurie, him and me havin' steaks for dinner. His medium, and mine damn near raw."

She stopped picking up the dishes and looked first at me and then at him. I doubt that she weighed seventy pounds, but her stare could have killed us both. At first she said nothing, but when she had finished picking up the dishes, she stared straight at Ernie and said, "Eatin' steak with a jailbud." She spun on her heel and was gone.

"I don't think she approves of me," I said.

Ernie broke out in a loud peal of gross phlegmy laughter. I stared at him. He as abruptly stopped. "Goddam niggers," he spat. "Her and Sorry think they're somep'm just cause they keep the jail instead of bein' in it."

"Sounds to me like that is something." I said. "The way things seem to be run around here."

"Shit," said Ernie. "That's the way ever'body around here is. Ever'body thinks the little old things they do is so damn great. Ole Beard and his trotline; Sorry and Laurie and their jail; Mist Collins always off huntin'. You know what I mean?"

"Huh," I said. "Don't you do anything?"

"What's to do?" he said.

I said nothing.

"I mean, I just get so lonesome, you know?"

"Yeah," I said, "I guess. What about Ole Beard?"

"Shhh—" he snarled. "That so-and-so can step to hell far as I'm concerned."

"You don't get along with him?"

"I get along with him. That don't mean I like him." Then viciously, "I hate his guts is what it means."

"What for?"

"Shhh—" He spat. Then he went on in a different tone. "I think he's jealous cause I's the one Mist Collins allus went huntin' with," he said. "I mean, he never read a verse of Bible in his life till Mist Collins come back, tellin' e'body he's a preacha and all. Then Ole Beard starts a-prayin' and readin' his Bible ever'day. He ain't stopped yet, and you know why?"

"Why?"

"Cause he ain't been around Mist Collins enough since then to know Mist Collins ain't a preacha no more."

"And this Collins fellow is always off in the woods."

Ernie nodded.

"What does he do?"

"Hunts and prays."

"Jesus," I said. "I don't see why you don't leave."

Ernie said nothing.

"Does anybody ever go out at all?" I said.

"Mist Collins. Don't nobody ever know when though."

"Could you leave if you wanted to?"

"I s'pose so," he said, slightly irritated. "Hell, how'm I s'posed to know? I doubt anybody'd know where to go if they did leave."

"You wouldn't?"

He shook his head.

"You never tried?"

"Once," he said.

"What happened?"

He poked his lip out and stared at the bed. "I stole a skiff and floated down the river to Baton Rouge," he said. "Got throwed in jail the first night I's there." He stared at me. "I ain't never been in jail here."

"So how'd you get back?"

"Quick as I got out, I jumped on some barges headed upriver. Swum ashore from that bend out yonder. That's how I bust my knee—landed on a log when I jumped off the barge."

"And you swam ashore with a busted knee?" I said.

He nodded. "Laurie splinted it, but it set straight, and I ain't been able to bend it since."

"How far did you have to swim? How close do the boats come?"

"Clear the other side." He pointed. "It's shallow as hell near bout to the other bank."

"I see," I said. "That must have been before you got married."

He looked down and shook his head.

"After?"

"Nah."

"You weren't running away from her?" I chuckled.

"No!" he exploded. For one brief instant, he glared hatred at me. "Naw," he said, "I wadn' runnin' away from her."

"She's dead though," I said.

"Yeah," he said, "she's dead," as though explaining his outburst.

"How long ago?"

"Must be about five years." He looked back up.

"And she was from here?"

"She was Ole Beard's daughter." He laughed bitterly.

"I can't believe you've been five years without a woman." I chuckled and shook my head. "Big healthy guy like you!"

He nodded.

"That must be rough."

"Goddam right."

"I'd think that would be enough reason to want to leave right there."

He said nothing.

"Don't you get mighty horny or lonesome or anything?"

"What of it?" he said.

"I don't know. I just mean—"

"Look, if I was to go out, I wouldn't marry another one of 'em for anything."

"You wouldn't?"

"I'd fuck 'em right and left, and marry none of 'em."

"Why so?"

"Cause sure as I did, she'd die on me."

"What makes you say that?"

"She just would is all."

"Why? How did the other one die?"

"She's havin' a baby."

"Well, don't you know that out there there's doctors that keep that from happening? I can be that kind myself, if I have to."

"It don't matter. She'd die of something."

"Why do you say that?"

He said nothing. He sat up and looked down at his hands.

"What's wrong?" I said.

He bit his lip. "Mist Collins said so."

"What? What did he say?"

"He said it was cause I run away. That was why she died."

"What are you talking about?"

"That's what he said. After she died, he said it was cause I run off."

"And how did he come up with such a tale as that?"

"Cause I run off and left her with the baby comin'."

"And how did that kill her?"

"Cause I run off to fuck," he said. He was crying. Huge wet tears rolled ridiculously down his dirty face. "All the time, before I took her for my wife, I ain't fucked nobody. Mist Collins, he run round and fuck niggers when we's fifteen years old. Ole Beard fuck his wife and the niggers too. But not me. My old lady she told me it ain't as good when you're married if you do it before." He spoke through heavy sobs. "Shit!" He spat. "Me breakin' down like this." He shook his head and stopped crying. He sat staring at me with the tears standing all over his face.

"So what happened?" I said.

"So we got married," he said. "Me and Mary."

"Mary Beard," I said.

"Mary Beard, hell!" he said. "Mary Barber. She's my goddam wife."

"Right," I said.

"And she was so pretty. It nearly killed me just lookin' at her."

"So what happened?" I said.

He looked away. Then he looked back, rubbing his hands over his face and smearing the tears around. "She didn' like it," he said.

"Didn't like what? You?"

"Fuckin'," he said.

"Most women don't right at first."

"That's what Laurie said," he said. "But after what my old lady told me, I didn' believe nobody."

"Huh."

"Anyhow, to beat all, we got a baby comin' from the little bit we did do. And ole Miz Beard tells her I can't fuck her at all till the baby comes."

"Well, now, that wasn't true," I said.

"I ain't surprised," Ernie said. "Way they poisoned her against me."

"So what then?" I said.

"I's goin' crazy," he said. "I thought about the niggers. But then I thought about all that time I waited, and I knew I wadn' goan go to no nigger now. So I remember I heard Mist Collins say one time they's places on the outside that sell fuckin' for money. Mary stayin' at Miz Beard's half the time anyway. I figgered she owed me somep'm for the way she kep' Mary upset alla time. So I stole a dollar and a half of her money. Jump that boat to Baton Rouge. When I come back, the Lord done took her. Mist Collins said it was cause I run off to fuck."

He sat still for a long time, chewing his lower lip. He wasn't crying now, but he was looking away, out the window toward the river. His eyes were huge and mud-colored, and each blink was pronounced.

Then he turned and stared viciously at me. "No sir," he exclaimed, "I'd never marry another of 'em in a million years. Mary's dead, and I'm goin' to hell. I'd fuck 'em right and left, and marry none. Fuck 'em all. Jest the hell with them."

That afternoon when Ole Beard came for me, Ernie made it a point to be gone to the outhouse, and I was sitting on the caved-in front porch waiting for Ole Beard. Even so, I never saw Ole Beard before he was right in front of me; it was as if he had just materialized out of the weeds. But I'd be damned if I'd let him see me look surprised. In my hand I had a hypodermic syringe full of coffee.

In his hand he had a .41 Colt revolver.

He looked as if he wanted to ask were Ernie was, but he didn't. Instead he pointed the gun at me. "Get up," he said.

I didn't move. "Ole Beard," I said, "I am going to turn you into a nigger." I squirted a little stream of black at his feet.

For once the vaguest hint of an expression came into his eyes.

"Now you listen to me a second," I said.

He wavered.

"You can kill me if you want to. There's no doubt about that. I mean there is just nothing in the world I could do to keep you from blowing my brains out if you decide that's what you want to do. But, Ole Beard, if you so much as look cross-eyed at me—now or ever again—whether you kill me or not—I am going to squirt this little thing on you, and you're going to be a nigger for the rest of your life."

His eyes drew as close together as shotgun barrels. "Ah doan b'lieve it," he said.

"Care to try it?" I said.

He raised the revolver. I raised the syringe.

He lowered the revolver. I kept the syringe pointed at his face.

"Now," I said, "I am ready to go back down to the jail, because I want to see and talk with Arnold. And you may come along to keep me from running away, if that's what you'd like to tell yourself, but mainly because you've got the key." I paused. "I'm ready when you are."

He studied me. "How fur," he said, "will that thang squirt?"

I looked at it, wondering the same thing myself. "Oh," I guessed, "about a mile." Then, looking directly into his eyes, "And it doesn't take but a drop."

By then Ernie had come around the house and was standing in the weeds, hitching up his overalls. Ole Beard glanced at him and back to me.

"Are you ready?" I said.

But I guess Ernie couldn't stand it any longer. He let go the overall straps and burst out laughing, and his pants fell off onto the ground. Then I laughed too, and squirted the coffee up in the air, so that it misted down on both Ole Beard and me. For one second Ole Beard jumped like he'd stepped on a snake trying to get out from under it; then I guess he realized what was going on because the world exploded in my face with coffee and powdered glass flying everywhere, and when I looked up, he had the still smoking .41 leveled at my nose.

"Ny gidup," he said.

I was unhinged. I laughed at him again. Then I threw the piece of the glass that I was still holding on the ground and got up. When we started walking, I started laughing again. I decided that if he was going to act like that about it, then I wasn't through with him yet.

"Ernie says you're quite a fisherman," I said as soon as we were out of Ernie's earshot.

He stopped. He threw me one glance, steely eyes again as close as the barrels of a shotgun.

"Guess he was mistaken," I said. I walked on and heard him start to follow.

Frogs and crickets were out in force for the preview of spring. The woods were electric with them. The mosquitoes were out too. I slapped and swatted, wondering why they weren't bothering Ole Beard. I turned and looked at him, and then I fancied that I knew. He looked bloodless. His mouth was small and very tight beneath the beard. It looked mean enough to bite the mosquitoes back. The sight made me flush with adrenaline.

"Said you were quite a lover too," I said.

He stopped walking, and I stopped and stared back at him.

"What Ernie say?"

"Aw"—I grinned, looking away—"he told me how you used to get all those niggers. Said how you used to just set the woods on fire."

I never saw him move. First thing I knew, the pistol butt was in my face, and I was sprawled backward in the road. I lay on my back, staring up at him. His mouth worked slowly, tensely, inside the beard. Once his tongue darted out and flicked back in. I touched my cheekbone. He hadn't hit me with the butt; he had simply shoved. There was no mark. I stared up at him, and for an instant I thought of jumping him. But where was there to go? Besides I knew he'd shoot me if I tried; I didn't have a chance. I lay in the road, breathing heavily, chewing my lip.

"Get up!" he said. I got up.

He prodded me with the muzzle of the cocked pistol, and we started walking toward the jail.

Then my stomach flushed cold. Something inside me drew up, trembling with fear or rage or both. I clenched and unclenched my fists. I wheeled on Ole Beard.

He recoiled, raising the pistol.

I stared at him. "Friend," I said, "I'm not sure just how, right now, but you're gonna pay for that."

"You goddam jailbird," he said.

"Jailbird? I've never been in jail before in my life. Who do you think you're talking to?"

"Nobody," he said. "Exactly nobody."

I stared at him for a long second.

"Walk," he said.

I turned and started walking.

The gravel-throated frogs were thick in the road-edge ditches. They made the only sound anywhere. The day was too hot for March. The wet heat bore down on the road. Suddenly the thought of spending the night in that stinking jail with Arnold was very unpleasant. The jail was black and squat at the end of the road.

I stepped up to the door and opened it myself. Then I stopped. Ole Beard jammed the pistol in my ribs, but still I didn't move. Anna was in the room.

"Move," Ole Beard said. I stepped aside. He looked in beside me.

It was very dark inside the jail. It took a long minute for my eyes to adjust. The smell was strong in the stagnant air.

Arnold was behind the bars, and the girl was sitting on the floor in front of him. She was holding a banjo, as though frozen in the act of playing it. She and Arnold stared at us in the door.

"Anna," said Ole Beard, "get up."

She did not move. Arnold was staring at Ole Beard.

"Get up and get back," Ole Beard repeated.

Anna glanced from him to Arnold and back.

"What's the matter? You jealous of that too?" I blurted.

All three of them looked at me.

I said nothing.

Ole Beard stepped suddenly forward, brandishing the pistol. He grabbed Anna by the shoulder. She let out an animal cry as he dragged her to her feet. The banjo crashed to the floor, ungodly loud in the close room. Arnold jumped to his feet.

Ole Beard held Anna by the shoulder, staring from her to Arnold and back. A low feral wail escaped Anna's throat. Ole Beard's face was calculating; it showed no trace of fear. He spun Anna around so that she faced him. Arnold shook the bars. "You git outa here," Ole Beard said to Anna. He pushed her toward the door, but she did not move. "You want me tell Mist Collins? He'll whup the daylights out of you." The low wail rose to a sob, a passion. He snatched her shoulder again, and her head spun away from him. She stared at the floor.

I stood in the door, clenching and unclenching my fists.

Ole Beard pointed the gun at me. "Move," he said. "Back inside." He gestured with the pistol.

I wiped my mouth with my hand. I moved.

He began dragging Anna toward the door, holding the gun on me. She jerked and bucked like a colt. She avoided his face. Beneath the beard, his expression never seemed to change.

Arnold was standing, rattling the bars. His eyes were wide and wild. His face had flushed to the color of an Indian's.

I stepped cautiously aside to let Ole Beard pass. I never took my eyes from the pistol, and he never took his eyes off me.

When he got to the door, he shoved Anna outside. He slammed the door behind her and wheeled on me. "Now move!" he shouted. "Go! Git on ovah there."

I sidled slowly in the direction of the cell door. Arnold was behind it, holding onto its bars.

"Now, you," Ole Beard snapped, pointing the gun at Arnold. "Get back! Get away from that door."

Arnold rattled the bars and stood his ground.

Ole Beard was the fastest man I've ever seen. The bars crashed like a thousand bells as he slammed the gun butt against Arnold's fingers and had the muzzle trained on me before I knew what he had done. Arnold was down in the back of the cell, but he was not looking at his hand. He was still looking at Ole Beard.

Ole Beard dug in his pocket and produced a key. He glanced from me to Arnold and back, carefully inserting the key in the Slage. I could see Arnold, not moving but tensing. Arnold's eyes were trained on the revolver. Slowly Ole Beard opened the door. He played the revolver between Arnold and me.

"Now get in there," he said very softly.

"Make me," I said.

He raised the revolver and pointed it at my face.

Then Arnold leapt forward, dove head-on into Beard's groin. The pistol exploded, and I was still alive. Ole Beard and Arnold went down together on the floor, scrabbling for the gun. I picked it up and swung it, uncocked, at Ole Beard's head, missing and grazing his shoulder. Arnold and Ole Beard rolled over and over on the floor of the jail. Arnold was bigger, but Ole Beard seemed almost impossible to hold. Time and again Arnold got above him and bore down with his weight, and every time Ole Beard squirmed loose to punish Arnold's stomach and short ribs with his small, sharp fists.

I didn't know what to do. Twice I tried to kick Ole Beard in the head, but once I missed completely, and the other time I got Arnold in the ass.

Then Ole Beard came loose from the pile. He was up and backing away from both of us while Arnold scrambled to his feet. Ole Beard dug in his pocket and came out with a case knife, which when he got it open, was nearly a foot long. I looked stupidly at the gun in my hand, and Arnold snatched it from me.

But in that second, Ole Beard came for him with the knife, ripping Arnold's shirtsleeve and bringing a thin line of blood down his arm. Arnold had the gun, but Ole Beard had his wrist, and Arnold's other hand was holding Ole Beard's knife arm. They were standing now, and Arnold had the size and strength. He bore the smaller man backward, bending him across the table. Ole Beard's forehead was turning blue. His mouth drew open, but no sound escaped. I was edging toward the banjo.

But then Ole Beard got his knee in Arnold's groin. He seemed to hold it there a second, testing, while a look of horror crossed Arnold's face. Then he shoved, and Arnold bawled with pain. He fell heavily backward against the wall, and the gun clattered to the floor. Ole Beard stood still for an instant, breathing, then moved for the gun.

I never could fight hand to hand, but give me a stick, anything like a baseball bat, and I feel better. In that instant I imagined Ole Beard's head as a high, inside curve, cocked the banjo, and stepped into it. The sound of his head against the resonator was deafening.

He didn't fall immediately. A look of shock came into his face, and he turned and looked at me as though he had forgotten all about the gun. His eyes were close again, like the shotgun barrels, but more amazed than threatening. He staggered, staring at me, seemingly unable to take those eyes off my face. So I cocked the broken banjo and hit him again, right across the gut. Blood was soaking through his hair as he slumped to the floor. He fell to one knee first, then backward on the floor, eyes still open, staring up at me.

Now Arnold was back up. He had the gun and was walking bowlegged toward us with it, trying to cock it with shaking hands. "Arnold, for God's sake, don't!" I yelled, trying to grab the gun.

"Fuck you, Fargus." He pushed me aside.

I grabbed the banjo again and swung it at the gun. The gun flew like a line drive into the wall. Arnold stared at his open hands. He turned on me. I brandished the banjo. "Arnold, for God's sake, that's murder." He stared at me and I held the banjo. Then Ole Beard moved, and both of us faced him.

Ole Beard's head lay in a pool of blood, and he was trying to get up. For a second both of us just looked at him. Then Arnold drew back his right foot. Ole Beard was looking at us both, struggling up onto his elbows. Arnold's boot shot forward, heavily and perfectly aimed, into Ole Beard's crotch.

Ole Beard's eyes rolled backward into his skull. The breath escaped him, and he settled back onto the floor, covering the place with his hands. Arnold and I stared. No one spoke.

Then the eyes came back onto us. Ole Beard tried to get his elbows under him again, and Arnold slammed the boot back into his crotch.

"Quit it!" I yelled at Arnold. He turned and glared at me. I held up the banjo, breathing through my teeth.

Arnold turned, stalked to the jail, went inside, and slammed the door.

I stood over Ole Beard, holding the banjo. Then Anna looked inside. She looked from Ole Beard to Arnold to me. She stepped inside the door, her eyes fixed on Ole Beard. I threw down the banjo and slumped onto the floor. Anna crept forward, staring at Ole Beard. She reached out her arm, seeming to want to touch him. A flush was in her cheeks, and her breast rose and fell with her breathing. I buried my eyes in my sleeve.

Then "Fargus!" Arnold yelled. I looked up; Ole Beard had gotten the gun. He was still lying on the floor, and he had it in his left hand. It seemed a struggle even for him to draw it to himself. His right hand was holding his groin. No one moved. No one spoke.

Ole Beard closed his eyes for several seconds, seemingly trying to swallow. Anna stared transfixed, her breast rising and falling, the low animal wail escaping her throat. Ole Beard turned the gun in his left wrist. He pointed the muzzle at his head, cocked the hammer, and fired.

It took me a long second even to get myself together enough to take in the picture. When I did, the first thing I saw was the blood. It was everywhere—a feast, an orgy for my eyes. Something inside me balanced delicately between nausea and ecstasy—and then there flitted crazily through my mind the image of what I would have done at almost any other time in my life: I'd have bent over and examined Ole Beard!

And that was mad—because if I ever saw a dead man in my life, he was dead. No, he wasn't dead—that wasn't the word. He was demolished. He was everywhere. On my pants. On the floor. On the wall.

Then suddenly I had to bend over for a different reason. I started vomiting, and once I started, I couldn't stop. I don't know how long it went on, but I do know that while I was doing it, I thought I was going to die. It felt like my entire gastrorespiratory complex was turning inside out and spilling on top of him, and when I finally got up, I felt like he looked. I staggered to the desk chair and fell into it, and I sat there for another time I couldn't measure.

The thing that happened next was the sound. It was Anna—her song. Her low, animal painsong. Her death song. The same song the maid had sung on the kitchen floor. Wordless. Tuneless. Almost casual. She moved, and Arnold rose to the bars and waited for her.

She went first to Ole Beard and bent over him singing more deeply, stronger. Her hair brushed the bloody, blown-out place in the side of his head, and she dipped her hands in the blood. Then she rose and went to Arnold. Arnold met her, and she touched him through the bars with her bloody hands.

I stared. Then I ran.

4

That night I had a dream straight out of Dante's Hell. There was this rocky rolling piece of ground, nowhere in particular but all in shades of green and battleship gray, and there were all these naked people walking around on it. And the thing that they all had in common was broken bones. Every one of them had some kind of an unset, unhealed fracture, and they were all walking around and around, looking for somebody to do something about it.

I slept at Ernie's house. He let me after I told him about Arnold and Ole Beard and about my passing Sorry on the way out of the jail who was apologizing to trees and chickens and who apologized to me, and then called me a damn jailbud, and then ran inside the jail and screamed. All Ernie said when I finished was, "Well, Mist Collins be back tamarra then, I reckon."

I started to ask him why. Would he have heard the shot or what? But I couldn't think of any reasonable alternative possibility. It just didn't fit the pattern of the way things had been going that the reason he would be coming back was that he had heard the shot. So, instead, I asked Ernie why he hadn't come when he heard it. "My foot," he said. At that point, completely against my will, a brief burst of giggles escaped me and as quickly stopped.

"What's the matter with you?" Ernie said.

"I mean, this is just crazy," I said. "I mean here this man's just shot himself and—and—you just sit there talking about your foot."

"I don't wanna see him," Ernie said. "I don't want no part in Ole Beard's dyin'."

"Well, doesn't it disturb you or anything?"

"Disturb me?"

"Well, my God, what kind of a place is this?"

"Just who in the hell do you think you are?" he screamed.

I said nothing.

He stared at his injured foot, absently picking at the bandage. His heavy, stubble-rough jaws were slowly, silently, working.

I got up, stamped across the room, and began digging in the pack for something to smoke, found my pipe, stuffed it, tried to light it, and got a mouth full of condensation. Vowing to smoke it anyway, I knocked the tobacco out, took the pipe apart, cleaned it on a fresh undershirt, put it back together, restuffed it, lit up, then sat erect, furiously exhaling the too hot clouds of thick smoke.

"How do you know Collins is coming back tomorrow?" I demanded.

"I been knowin' him too long not to know when he be back," he muttered, still picking at the bandage.

"Well, what is it? You don't even care about Ole Beard?"

"Don't care? You lissen here, Doc, don't you go messin' with me an' Ole Beard, cause what we got between us ain't nobody else's business, you hear?"

"Who's messing?"

"There ain't but one man I ever hated in my entire life, and that was him. You know what he used to do? He used to get Mary off in the woods and tell her how if she ever let a man fuck with her, there was a water moccasin in his britches that would bite her and bite her till she died, and so she never did like fuckin', even the few times we could do it, and then when she died, he acted like that really was why."

"And that's why you wanted to stay away?"

"It's cause if I seen him I'd be glad he's dead," he said.

"Oh, my God," I said.

So I went to bed and had that dream. There was one thing I never got used to during the whole time I was in med school—broken bones. Whenever I came into contact with a patient who had a fracture, I'd get a kind of ache and have the same flesh-crawling feeling you get when you hear someone scratch a dusty chalkboard. When I was in med school, I gritted my teeth and took it. Since then, I've avoided it; you don't run into many broken bones diagnosing yeast infections.

But that night, everybody's bones were broken. Elbows swiveled 360 degrees. Legs had three joints. People crawled and writhed all over each other, looking for a doctor, and I was running, trying to get away from them, but they were everywhere. No matter how far or how much I ran, I was running through these people.

The thing that woke me was the sound of an engine. I sat up on the floor and looked around; it took me a minute to get out of the dream and get my bearings back. Then I knew what it was—an airplane. I got up and went outside, careful not to wake Ernie.

I couldn't see the airplane through the trees, but I could hear it very plainly. It was low, under not much power. I started running through the woods, looking for a clearing to try and make some kind of signal. Surely they would have seen our plane. Surely they would land and make some kind of a search when they saw it in the lake. But, no, they couldn't land in the lake without a helicopter because of the stumps.

I was running even harder. The vines were catching me, and twice I fell. They'd land in the river then. They'd see the plane, and then come around and land in the river. But I had no idea how far the plane was from the river. Sometimes those lakes could be miles away, and nobody would think there could be any passable overland route.

The engine was going away, back in the direction of the other side of the river. I stopped running. I was panting, breathless, drenched in sweat and dew. My pants were ripped from the vines. My arms and face were cut. I sat back against a tree trunk to try and catch my wind.

Then for the first time I stopped and looked at the day. The weather was changing again. For four days now, the days had been sharp and clear and hard, the wind from the south blowing hard and rife, the kind of March days that burn your lips. But now the wind was calm. There was a faint, high, thin, even overcast. I knew what was happening. Winter was by no means dead. Another cold front was moving down from the north, and at the moment it was holding the south wind at a standoff. But that wouldn't last. This early, the cold front would have more strength. The cold air would come barging down and meet the hot wind head on, and there would be another storm like the one that made us crash. But now the air—the space between the earth and the high, thin clouds—was vacant, hollow, hot. Nothing stirred. No leaf moved. No bird chirped or fluttered. Far in the distance I could distinctly identify a squirrel changing trees.

I stood up after my breath came back. I looked all around, then back in the direction from which I had approached the tree. There was nothing, no sign of anything familiar. "Son of a gun," I said out loud. I moved my arms where they were ripped, then touched the scratches on my face. I walked around the tree, staring incredulously at it. "Well, I'll be damned," I said again. "It can't be that far."

I started back walking in the direction from which I had reached the tree, looking for some sign, some footprint, or something that looked familiar. But there was nothing. I hadn't seen anything because I had been looking up through the trees, and I didn't want to keep walking that way because I remembered that I had been zigzagging a whole lot while I was running, looking for some kind of clearing.

Then I saw a briar thicket that I could have sworn I remembered approaching from just "that" particular direction. I struck out that way, and then I looked back to see if the briar thicket was in the proper relation to the tree where I had stopped. I stood perfectly still, looking. I couldn't tell whether the tree where I stopped was the hickory on top of that bluff, or the oak on top of that other one. Why didn't I make sure of that before I left?

What was it all the woodsmen's manuals said you were supposed to do when you got lost? Circle? No, that was what lost people always ended up doing. But what were you supposed to do? Better yet, what was I supposed to do?

I started walking again, back in the direction from which I thought I had tripped over the briars. Then away off to the right I thought I saw a tree that I remembered looking up through, trying to catch sight of the plane. I hurried over to it and looked up through the branches to see if it looked the same. It was close. I moved around under it, trying to get the right perspective. I got it. Yes, I was sure I had looked up through this same tree. Then I stood back, trying to remember which direction I had been coming from. I thought I had it, and I started walking.

I walked for about five minutes, looking for something else that seemed familiar. I couldn't find anything. The woods were unutterably huge. Giant stands of heavy, massive oaks and hickorys and the small, thick clumps of gums enclosed my sight. Still nothing moved except myself. I stood still, looking for a long time. Then I shifted my weight from one foot to the other, and the sound was outrageously loud, it sounded once when I moved and then came back on me, echoing again and again in my mind. I looked around again. What to do? What had I been doing? I had been going back in the direction from which I thought I had approached that one particular tree. I had been going *that* way. So I set off that way again. I was walking hard now, taking giant, fast, heavy steps. The ground was soft and wet, sloping downward. All around me the leaves and branches, the canebrakes and the vines, the slow, rolling, loamy earth of the forest floor, seemed to grow closer and closer, opening before me and closing behind me like water.

Don't panic, I thought, putting extra effort into my speed. Don't panic—that's what all the books say. Oh, yes, go in one direction, that's what else they say; go in one direction until you cross a path or a road. Well, that's what I was doing. I was going in one direction.

The land was sloping downward, getting softer the farther I

96

went. The honeysuckle and poison ivy of the bluffs were giving way to the thicker ferns and creepers of the swamp. Some places I had to turn to one side or the other to avoid a thicket so deep or so dense that I couldn't get through it. Every tree had the stuff—vine about as thick as a pencil with three leaves on every little stem, completely enclosing and hiding the trunk, reaching clear up to the first branches, tangled as densely as a mat and studded with thorns. Once I foundered in a place where it had completely filled and concealed a hole as deep as my leg, and out of it spurted a cottontail, bounding twice, and disappearing like magic before my eyes.

Sweat ringed my collar and armpits, and the mosquitoes found that and began whining about my ears. I flew into a rage, slapping and fighting at them, and I envisioned Ernie's shotgun barrel with all the mosquitoes in the world crowded inside, and in my mind I fired the gun and delightedly murdered every mosquito.

I kept walking. Down, down, sloped the land, the underbrush growing always thicker. I dodged more and more briar thickets, until at last I lost all track of the direction that I had been trying to keep. But keep walking, I thought, keep walking, and you're bound to come to something, a trail or something, one of those paths that you took going from the plane to Graceville. It seemed now that the creepers covered everything. There was no more ground, as such, but the bottom of the forest was the tangled mat of living barbed wire, the creepers. I no longer went where I wanted, dodging the creepers where I encountered them; I went where I could, anywhere I could walk on top of them, anywhere that they didn't cut me off completely.

But still the farther I went, the worse they got, so I tried to turn around, to get back out on higher ground where I could at least move. I tried to go back and retrace my steps, but I couldn't find them. Everywhere I stepped the vines gave way, and my feet disappeared into them, and when I pulled my feet out, the vines sprang back leaving no trace of my track. Everywhere I looked they surrounded me—thirty, forty, fifty feet up the dense tree trunks.

All of a sudden I began charging against them, lowering my shoulder like a fullback hitting the line. Thorns ripped into my neck and arms, and the vines gave a little, only to spring back and toss me into the thorny cushion of more vines. I struggled free and charged again, and the vines ripped and bound and dug in, and then sprang back, but this time they held, fastened in my shirt and neck and in the back of my hair. I went wild, thrashing and kicking, and when I came free, I fell over on my face into more vines with vines still hanging in my hair and skin and clothes.

And then I gave up. I just lay there, sweat and blood rolling down my face, more thorns in my skin than I could begin to count. I cried for a second, but it was just the frustration leaking out with no other escape now that I wasn't moving. Then I was completely still.

Far away, somewhere, I heard the first flat, dry, hollow clap of thunder. Still there was no wind, no stirring leaf, no flutter of bird wings.

But then there was a voice. "Having trouble?"

I froze. The heat in that vinebound hell had a second before been bearing in on me like a flatiron. In a split second's time I was freezing. Slowly, half reluctantly, I turned my head. And there, standing as though without weight on top of the vines, was a small, muscular man about my own age, with silverish blond hair, dressed exactly as I was, with a pack and a large, expensive-looking shotgun slung across his back. And directly behind him, standing likewise as though weightless on the vines, stood a brown, somnolent mule loaded with the carcasses of three deer.

"Robert Collins is my name," he said. "And yours?"

I swallowed, gulped air, and swallowed again. "Henry Fargus," I said, and then for some reason, "Dr. Henry Fargus."

"Well, Dr. Fargus, you seem to be having some difficulty."

I looked at myself, then back at him. "Yes," I said after a minute. "I got lost."

"It helps if you know the roads," he agreed.

"Uh"—I stared for a long minute at the vines under him—"Is that a road—that you're on right now?"

"Well," he said, "it's sort of a catwalk across the swamp."

"I see." For some reason I still hadn't stood up.

"I would suggest," he said, "that you go right around that tree. There's a little stream bed there that you can follow over to the catwalk, and then I'll drop you a rope."

"Right around that tree," I said.

He nodded.

I got up and made for the tree. In the time that I had been down, the scratches had stiffened. I fought into the vines again, progressing only inch by inch. Twice I turned and looked at Robert Collins. Neither time did he appear to have moved a muscle. Finally I got to the stream bed. It was a tunnel *under* the weeds, so that in the time I was in it I couldn't see him at all.

But when I reached the catwalk, he was standing directly over me with a heavy rope tied around the tree to which I could see that the catwalk was fastened. By then every muscle in me was screaming for relief, but I wouldn't let Robert Collins know it. I grabbed the rope and climbed it, hand over hand, and when I made the top he grabbed me under the armpits and helped me belly onto the splinter-ridden split logs of the walk.

I sat still for a long second, breathing, him standing over me with an expression of slight amusement on his round face. The mule, I could now see, had been blinded so that it would stand still on the walk. Its eyes had been completely removed, and I wondered who in that town had done it. "Do you have any water?" I said with as much self-possession as I could muster.

"A little," he said, disappearing from my sight because I was too tired to turn and watch him go as far as the mule. He returned with a leaky, almost flat, canvas water bag. I uncorked it, took a swallow, sat for a moment feeling funny, then vomited over the edge of the catwalk. Robert Collins said nothing. I still felt thirsty, so I took another swallow. This time it seemed as though it would stay down.

"Thank you," I said, handing him back his bag. "Are you heading back to town?"

"Yes," he said. "And you?"

I nodded, struggling to my feet. He replaced the bag on the mule. We began walking, my body crying outrage at every step.

And Robert Collins was smiling. He didn't ask me what I was doing on his island, didn't tell me whether he had seen the plane, but he walked with his head cocked slightly to one side, his shoulders slightly bowed, a little too much spring in his step, and that constant, wise, bemused smile.

We followed the precarious catwalk from tree to tree until the ground began to rise beneath it, and the vines began to thin, and

99

then we walked out onto the actual ground again, actual dirt where you could see the earth beneath the leaves and grass. Behind us and off to the left, I could see where the swamp turned and broadened, where the dark tannin-stained water flowed from beneath the vines, and the oaks and hickorys ended, and the cypress began. The water went as far as you could see; clear, it seemed, into the heart of the jungle itself.

"That water—" Robert Collins said.

I stopped, turned, and faced him.

"You see how brown it is?"

"Yes," I said.

"From here"—now he had stopped too, and was looking past me at the swamp—"from here it looks completely black, doesn't it? I mean, standing here and looking at it, you'd think you couldn't see through it. You'd think it would be perfectly black."

I nodded.

Then he moved, going to the mule and pushing its head toward a low hanging branch. "Come on," he said, "you want to see something?"

"Sure." I shrugged.

He wrapped the mule's lead rope around the branch, then watching me to make sure I was following, smiling at me as though wanting me to want to follow, he began walking rapidly toward where I could see a tiny foot trail leading away from the road and back down into the swamp. "Don't worry," he said. "There's no more vines."

So I followed him as he glanced alternately ahead along the down-sloping trail and back at me to make sure I wasn't having trouble. The trail wound lower and lower along the sloping bank for about forty or fifty yards, then came out parallel to the water's edge just a step above it.

"Here," he said, falling immediately to his hands and knees and leaning out above the water, "look down in there. Just look at·it. It isn't black at all; it's clear."

So I got down on my hands and knees beside him and leaned out over the water, staring down into it, and it was clear. It was clear and at the same time very dark, like looking through polarized glass where every color, every minute shade and every focus are pre-

100

served, and yet with a darkish sense of coolness and quietude. Dozens of crayfish crept unalarmed across the leaves which covered the bottom, and farther out I could see the shadows of heavy fish drifting sleepily just above the edge of the channel.

I turned to Robert Collins. "Why don't they spook?"

"The crayfish?"

"Yes."

"Because they're not afraid of us," he said. And then he broke into a laugh. "Why should they be? I'm not a Cajun. I don't eat crayfish. Do you?"

"Well, no," I said, "but I've just never seen crayfish so still—so close, I mean. I mean every time I ever saw one he was running from me. All I ever saw was the mud boil where he took off."

Robert Collins was still smiling, that same sad smile which he had kept too long the same to represent an ordinary expression of pleasure or contentment. "And have you ever seen any of these bass?" he said. "I mean the ones out of black water?"

I shook my head.

"Well, here," he said, "you're tired. You wait here a second, and I'll go back to the mule and get something. It'll only be a minute."

I shrugged, and he got up, disappearing, walking fast up the trail. I was tired. Every muscle craved not to move again. I leaned out slightly and looked back down into the water. The crayfish still hadn't moved. There was something fascinating about them, as though they weren't really there, or not in the same way that I was here. It was like every time I'd ever seen a crayfish before—up close, I mean—somebody had caught it and had been holding it, and the legs and pincers had been squirming and writhing and looking for a way to grab onto a finger, but here that wasn't possible. The crayfish couldn't grab you, didn't want to, and its legs and pincers became slender, delicate tendrils.

I leaned back up and over against a tree. Now I didn't mind being tired; I didn't need to move.

Robert Collins reappeared before I expected him carrying a fine, old, tonkin fly rod, the kind Arnold wished he had, but that you couldn't buy anymore, not over seven feet long and as alive as part of your arm. "Do you know how to use a fly rod?" he said.

"Not very well, I'm afraid. I have."

101

"Well, watch this. Then you can try. I bet you've never seen a bass like this before in your life."

So he stripped out a few yards of line and neatly rolled the small, homemade fly out across the black clear water, and it settled without even a ripple, perched seemingly without weight on the surface film, and rested. For a long moment he let it rest. Then he gave it the slightest twitch. I watched the greenish silhouettes beneath the surface. Slowly they began to turn and face the motionless bug. Robert Collins twitched it again. Then, almost before I saw the shape move, the diamond black surface erupted in a sheet of spray, and Robert Collins lofted his rod above his head, and the bass leapt and tailwalked across the water, then fell and leapt again and again, and he led it to the bank and picked it up and held it for me.

"See?" he said. "See what I mean?" He was trembling. His smile was the same, but huge.

"Yes," I said. "Yes, I see."

5

The big wood flames roared up from the top of the heaped-up logs, and the little blue methanol flames licked impishly among the sap-sputtering coals. It was black dark now, but our fire was huge, and it lit the jungle for a space as big around us as a house, a space leaping with monstrous shadows. We were now some measureless distance farther down the trail that paralleled the water. Robert Collins had not said where we were going, but I assumed that it was not back to Graceville. In any case, I had no desire to leave him and try and find my way alone.

He had hardly spoken again since he caught the fish. But the smile he had worn since the first time we spoke still hadn't changed. If anything, it had grown deeper and sadder. Now I looked at him across the fire. His eyes, though obviously not closed, were invisible beneath some quality of dark intuition that covered his face. In the firelight his face was round and ruddy with only a day's growth of beard. Without his gray hair, it might have been a boy's face; the fire gave it that kind of a glow.

He reached over and absently stirred the coals with a green stick. "Well," he said, as though we had been talking all day, "I used to have myself a fine island."

"Used to?" I said.

Then he looked at me. I said no more.

He stood up and unspitted the venison steak that had been charring over the blaze. We had mushrooms, which he had gathered, and watercress from the frigid spring that gurgled up through the sand just outside the firelight, and spring water to wash it down. We fell to eating in silence. When we had finished, he looked up again.

"You know," he said, "I started out to be a preacher."

I said nothing.

"I was raised here. I was born here and I grew up here, and my father was and his father before him, and I don't think the place has changed at all in three generations."

I still said nothing.

Part III

Robert Collins spent many weeks in the woods praying, so that when he came into Natchez he thought he knew what God wanted him to do. He preached on street corners until he had collected enough to buy a large tent. Then he pitched the tent on the edge of town, and there he formed the congregation that built him a white church on the hill just across from the town cemetery. During the whole time he ate no fish with scales and no birds with scaly feet.

Then he set about finding himself a wife. Ezra Farmer was the oldest and richest member of his congregation. During his life Ezra Farmer had been a member of almost every Protestant congregation in Natchez and had quit them all because he found none willing to take up arms against the evil which he saw about him. His daughter, Anna, was engaged to a big, handsome, red-faced, pleasure-loving man named Boyce Winston, who worked on the river and loved a drunken fight on Saturday nights. Ezra Farmer was the morose and powerful man behind the Farmer Bank, and he had not been out on the streets of the town for many years. The first time in those years that Ezra Farmer was seen on the streets was when he went to hear the Reverend Collins in the tent. The Reverend Collins seemed willing to take up arms, and Ezra Farmer was the driving force behind Collins' new church building. Then the Reverend Collins came and asked for his daughter, Anna, in marriage. Ezra Farmer thought for a long time about this, then had Boyce Winston fired and declared anathema in the city of Natchez, and he gave his daughter to Robert Collins for a wife.

For the first weeks of their marriage, Anna was very quiet. She performed her wifely duties as though she were serving some remote and powerful master. Then Robert Collins found the pale lip rouge hidden among her underthings. He seized her by the wrists and dragged her into the churchyard. He tied her hands above her head around a tree limb so that her toes barely touched the ground. Then he stripped her to the waist, viciously and methodically tearing off her clothes. He whipped her with his heavy, brass-bound belt, then cut her down, and left her in the dust to repent.

When Anna came back to Ezra Farmer's house and he saw what Reverend Collins had done, Farmer asked her why he had done it. She told him about the lipstick, and Farmer stared at his own powerful hands for a long time. Then he sent her back to be with her husband. Ezra Farmer went up into his attic and prayed all night. After that, he was once again a morose and powerful man who did not go out into the streets of Natchez for the rest of his life.

But without Ezra Farmer, Reverend Collins' church did not prosper. The people complained that Collins cared nothing for them, and Collins agreed: he cared for God, and it was their business to do the same. Then the Reverend Collins preached for a crusade of Christian knights to burn and wreck the establishments of every moonshiner and bootlegger in the county. It was to be on a Friday night, and Collins was ready with his shotgun, but no one came. The next Sunday the church was all but empty, and there was not enough collection for Collins and his wife to eat. He sent Anna back to her father's house, and went once again into the woods.

The first time he went back into the woods, he walked for five days straight in a giant circle and returned to his father-in-law's porch where he sat for two days, staring at the river. His mother-in-law asked him where he had been, and he told her that he had been waiting for a revelation. Then, on the third day, he went into the woods again, carrying only his shotgun and his fishline. He walked directly to that point along the river from which he could look across the water and see the land of his father from which he had fled. The day was autumn and the hint of chill was in the woods, and it was sitting there along the river that he had his vision.

He saw the land of his father in the autumn, and every leaf on the island was red and yellow, and there was death all around him. The entire island was like the giant red ball of a setting sun, and the year was as one gigantic dying day. There was deer killing and hog killing for winter meat, and the woods were full of blood and the voices of the dogs that coursed the deer. November was a dying.

But then December came to him, a death, and the island was no longer like a sun. The leaves were torn from the trees and driven into the ground by wind and sleet, and the naked limbs rattled like bones. It was night, hours before the dawn, and he saw himself moving along the river in a wooden skiff to a smaller island and hiding from it in a button willow thicket, hiding until the cold and the death crept into the thicket and got so close to him that he had to face it, clutching the shotgun like a suicide knife. This hunting was not for meat. It was death that he was hunting in the wind and sleet that killed the trees, and it was death that he was completing when he gunned the ducks.

The dawn came like a stillbirth, and he stood and blasted into the wind. The ducks rode the north wind that funneled through the river channel. The mallards, wood ducks, and canvasbacks ate up fifteen yards of wind with every wing beat and went screaming past his face. He shot, reloaded, stood, and shot again, and saw a back-broken drake wing over and go sailing with the wind across the channel. He reloaded again and shot, and finally caught a mallard flaring straight upstream, had him dead on, and the gun clapped and the mallard started falling, falling like forever, landing dry right at his feet without a feather turned, and snow sticking one flake at a time to his green head.

He sat in the boat with the gun across his lap, and he thought: I've done it; whatever it was I came here for, I've faced it, and I've done it.

That was when he heard it, not wings, not ducks, but a voice, one sky-high yelp. He looked up from his duck and saw the formation

106

of Canada geese spread against the blue scud like they owned the sky and wind and cold and death, like all death was their death, and they were the gods of snow and winter and death.

So he knew that he hadn't faced it; he hadn't done it. He hunkered in the boat, trying to get out of the wind, and pleading through the lurid little goose whistle on a string around his neck. The old lead gander heard and answered, came a little lower. The end geese, not as smart as he, would be in range if nothing flared them. The geese came sailing in above him, and he reached for his gun, and it was almost time, and then he was up, and he never even saw what it was that they did, never saw how they changed the way they were not-flapping their wings that carried them up into free air out of range. Sitting on the riverbank, Robert Collins saw himself, burning hot despite the wind, stand and fire off both barrels at the rising geese. Then he turned and reloaded and stood and fired again. The geese rose, disappeared, calling to each other in the scud.

Sitting on the riverbank, across from his father's land, his vision came to an end, and it was dark. Then he knew that he would not go back to Natchez unless it was to get his wife in such time as he could leave this land which was not the land of his father from which he had fled.

1

Robert Collins stopped talking. He looked directly at me now, intently studying my face. I said nothing. I hoped that my face proclaimed nothing, neither interest nor boredom. The blind mule urinated loudly somewhere outside the firelight. Then Robert Collins looked away.

"Do you by any chance," I asked him, "have anything that can be smoked?"

"I have some tobacco," he said. "But—" He looked at my face. I cocked my head and said nothing more. "Would you like to share my pipe?" he said quietly.

"I would," I said.

He got up and disappeared in the direction of the mule.

The elements, the north and south winds, still held their standoff. You could feel it. The air was still, vacant, and hollow. The smoke from the campfire rose straight up, then spread evenly outward from the updraft and fell back to the earth. You could feel the fronts, as though they were circling each other with you in the middle, sizing each other up before coming to death blows. In the north there was still the winter, the iron-hard sleet, the vicious wind. And in the south there was the hot, dank Gulf wind with the power of life and rebirth out of the hard death of winter. They circled with me in the middle, concealing nothing, preparing for the altercation.

Robert Collins returned with the pipe. He stuffed it meticulously, pinch by pinch, then rubbed off all the flakes from the edge of the bowl. He stirred the coals with a dry twig. He uncovered one of the hottest coals and held the twig against it until the twig caught fire. Then he lit the pipe—carefully, evenly, deeply, all around and took one long, tentative puff still holding the burning twig. He nodded and threw the twig back into the fire and handed me the pipe. I took it and inhaled deeply, holding it while the nicotine was absorbed and while it anesthetized my tensed muscles. Then I nodded and handed it back. He moved closer so we could pass it without getting up.

He began talking again, and an urgency came into his voice.

Robert Collins considered disappearing into the world, becoming nameless and as nondescript as possible, which, he knew, was a way of wanting to die without facing death. He also considered becoming a celibate priest, remaining alone forever in his cell which, he knew, was another way of wanting the same thing. But what he did was to walk.

He walked through the thin woods and the Codifer Hills, south of Natchez, but the woods there vexed his spirit. For when Robert Collins thought of woods, he thought of something bigger and wilder than any mere trees and water. He believed in trees and water in the way that the Jews believed in the ark of the covenant: Not that God was in the ark, but all of God was there that they could ever touch. But the thin, logged-out woods and Codifer Hills and the waters lined with fishermen and beer bottles were a poor ark, and Robert Collins found in them and in himself a poor spirit. He was lonely for the land of his father.

He walked for many days, feeling the ground as filth beneath him, feeling the filth of it on his body, so that there was no place where he could rest and no water in which he felt that he could wash. He felt hunted and driven by the place's filth. Then he grew hungry. He could go for many days without food, but one day the need came on him like a desperation. He found a deer trail and followed it all that day until at dusk it led into a briar thicket. He hid that night and slept a little, but was ready with his shotgun at daylight.

At daybreak the smoky shapes emerged among the curtains of mist. They tripped on neat hooves back along the trail. Robert Collins picked out the smallest; the shotgun roared outrage in the quiet dawn, and the other shapes vanished. But as he approached the carcass he noticed something, a brass tag, on the spike buck's ear. He knelt and read it: State Game and Fish; No. 357 . . . . He left the deer where it lay and fled. He fled for four days straight until once more hunger overtook him.

That night he stole into a town and took food from a grocery store—apples and beef in a can. He ate it in the dark, in a hollow where someone had dumped a load of garbage. He slept that night among the garbage, but when the daylight woke him, he felt repulsed by his gun. That day he walked straight to the spot along the river which was across from the land of his father, and there hid his gun, his fishline, and his ammunition. He kept walking.

After that, he never camped. He took food where he could find it and slept where he dropped. And he began to feel that there were people following him. At first they were indefinite people, personifications of the filth of the ground. But then they were people of the towns, the people from whom he had stolen.

By this time there was very little of the land of the Codifer Hills through which he had not walked. Time and again he found himself by accident in a place where he had already been, and the thought of this was like a desperation to him. When he dropped, he dreamed the terror of meeting himself in the woods. He felt a division growing in himself. There was the *I* of him which seemed to float above the *me*. The *I* had quit caring about the walking and the meager food he stole. The *I* quit caring whether he starved or the people caught him and threw him into one of their smelly little jails. The *I* floated above the *me*, and to it the *me* looked like a corpse. But the *me* drove desperately on. The *me* starved, stole food, and was still hungry. The *me* heard the townspeople following it, moving through the brush. Everytime the *me* stopped moving, it went wild. Robert Collins walked a long way and many days, and one evening at twilight something happened that brought his walking to an end.

It was November. The deer were losing their velvet and growing hot for the rut. The nights were getting the kind of clear, crystalline chill that makes the stars seem twice as close. The leaves were almost gone.

The sunset stopped his walking. There was the feeling of something loose in the land, and the clouds were building up around the sunset, the heavy ones filled with violent pink and the scud cupped out above the woods like the shiny inside of a mussel shell. Robert Collins looked around himself. He was by a creek, a little draw with a black water trickle up its middle. Then a feeling crept up his spine. He should have known this creek; he'd walked this way before. Yet, it seemed to him like no other place in the Codifer Hills. The woods were close, dark, and cold, and the air was wet and dangerous. The *I* seemed once more to occupy his hands and legs and eyes. He started walking up along the little creek.

And the way he walked was different. He was walking away from nothing, but toward something. He felt suddenly at home. Yet he had no idea where he was or where he was going. He walked quietly through the dense dangerous trees.

All this went through his mind, and still he had no notion why, until he heard, up ahead and through the trees, that first mallard hen rare back her head and cut her absurd, highball quack-quack-quack—and then he knew. It was getting darker, and he was getting closer, and he knew where he was going, so he started to be very careful walking down along the creek. He knew then that the creek was running out of a beaver pond, and he knew what he would find when he got there. He moved very slowly in the quiet, rough plaster mud along the creek. They would be there if he was quiet. There would be ducks there at least this once. He all but crawled.

And now the light was perfect. The sky was blazing, but there was no light on the ground. He moved by instinct in among the trees, and he could hear the ducks, burning the air above him. The draw widened out, and he could hear the running water of the beaver dam ahead. Behind the dam the ducks would be ganged up in the beaver pond, feeding on acorns and cypress boles. And he knew that he could come upon them from below, the last direction from which they would expect danger.

He moved as though life depended on it—not his life, but the whole world's: Everything that kept the world in its proper perspective; that made evil, evil, and good, good; and that made wildness and winter and death a thing worth having and fighting against.

Then he came to the dam and the little trickle of water cascading down over the logs. He hovered up against the logs for a long second, not resting, not because he was tired, but just to get his thoughts straight before he looked. Then he looked.

The pond was covered with gabbling, preening ducks, brown bodies and bright ones with erect green heads. The mallards were still landing, feathering their wings for no lift and flattening their bodies against the wind for brakes and control, and at the last second flailing up a small tornado until they lit without raising a ripple on the water itself. And the teal came boiling across the water in a whirling, twinkling cloud, swirling up and plopping down all at once, and the widgeons and pintails were sitting on the water, pecking at each other and feeding on the acorns and cypress boles. But the proudest ducks of all, the wood ducks, would not even alight. They weren't big and powerful like the mallards, or even fast like the teal, but they flew with heads erect, colors flaming in the sunset. Pairs of a hen and a drake crossed and recrossed the pond, screaming derision to the woods, screaming that they were wood ducks to every other creature on the lake.

The sky was high, thin, and transparent in the last of the light. Robert Collins clung to the logs of the beaver dam, not even knowing where he was.

That was when he heard the first goose. The ducks were settling by then, mallards against the far bank, and teal boiling and resettling as the light dimmed. The wood ducks were perching in trees. Robert Collins hunkered up against the logs, and for an instant the *I* and the *me* reseparated; he heard between them his thoughts saying, "This can't be real. I have covered every acre of these Codifer Hills, and this place is not real." But then the *I* and *me* reintegrated thinking, "No. This is real," the *I* and *me*, whole, swelling and filling the space above the pond. Robert Collins felt himself as the whole woods and the water and the winter light, the ducks living inside him, settling to the surface of the pond. And when the last duck had settled, he felt himself still hanging in the winter light like the red cast that hangs in a jar of water and red clay when the clay has settled out. He thought, "This is real. This is more real than all churches, and all towns, and all tagged deer." That was when he heard the first goose, the first sky-high yelp. He turned his eyes to the sky, and there splayed against the transparence were eighteen Canada honkers, wings set, necks out, gliding, circling, coming to the pond. He froze.

He hoped that his limbs would look just like the logs. He hoped that the ground was dark enough so that he could not be seen. He thought that perhaps they were not real geese and that maybe they wouldn't know he was there whether they saw him or heard him or smelled him or not. He froze and watched them come. He watched them from the size of ducks to the size of eagles to the size of bombers. He watched until they hung above the water with their feet dangling, settling, end geese first and then the older, bigger ones near the middle. Finally the big old frazzle-faced gander who had been the leader of the flock set down, and all the geese had their heads straight up, and all the ducks were quiet. Robert Collins stared straight at the gander, and he would have sworn the gander was staring straight at him.

Long seconds passed. Robert Collins stared at the long black neck and felt his own neck craning above the logs. His gaze bored into the gander's eyes, and he felt unable to shoot the gander. He thought, "Here I am, not twenty feet from the one of all creatures that nearly made me swear off shooting creatures and want to shoot myself; and I don't think that I am going to be able to shoot it." Neither of them moved.

But then the old lady goose, the gander's mate, swam up to the gander and started pecking at his tail feathers. The gander turned and hissed at her, but she kept pecking at him. Suddenly the gander clouted her in the back of the head with his beak. She slunk away, and the gander returned to face Robert Collins. "He's too old to need her," Robert Collins thought. "I bet his cods have dried up." The question of whether he was hidden was gone from Robert Collins' mind. Now all he thought was, "Just what is it he sees?"

Robert Collins thought of all the miles he had walked through empty, filthy woods, and all the times he had been hungry no matter what he ate. He thought of how the gander must feel, returning every year to look for a place where he would not have to associate with tagged deer. Robert Collins thought about the land of his father and about his own duck island. He thought of how they too might someday be like these woods and how someday someone might find his duck island and build a blind and be there, on some kind of a first legal shooting day to shoot a banded duck and feel a hero for turning in the tag.

Robert Collins looked once more at the goose. The goose was staring straight at him. Its mate was hovering behind, pretending to preen some infinitesimal speck from her feathers. Robert Collins could tell that she was afraid, but that she was afraid to show it. So he tensed and got ready.

He was not waiting now, and still the time before he moved seemed endless. He wondered how it would be in that one instant that always passes between the time the trigger gives and the time you see what has happened. "It's going to be a warp," he thought, "like the instant before the Second Coming." They stared straight on. The old lady swam around in front and looked desperately at the gander. The gander ignored her. The old lady let out a yelp and made as though to take off from the pond. The ducks boiled up before her until she settled against the far bank. And the gander and Robert Collins ignored all of this. Then Robert Collins felt himself moving.

When he moved, the duck wings gasped like an awestruck

113

crowd. Then he was up, and the gander still had not moved. Ducks were clawing for space, and the beaver logs were flying from beneath his feet, and it should have come, should have warped, and then he realized—he did not have his gun.

2

That night Robert Collins did not try to sleep in the Codifer Hills. He walked to the place along the river where he had hidden his shotgun and ammunition. He got out his shells and counted them, separating the deer shells, the buck and ball, from the duck and goose shells. He put the deer shells back, then separated the duck and goose shells into different pockets, and he cleaned his gun. He did these things without thinking of them. His thought seemed suspended. He had left it hanging in the twilight above the pond and staring into the gander's eyes. He built no fire and used no light. He did everything by feel, then left that place in the blackest dark without ever having seen it and without ever hoping to see it again.

In the sky the clouds had made a solid cover. The wind was up and blowing steadily above the trees. As he made his way back through the woods, he could not feel the wind above the trees, but he could hear it. And he could see absolutely nothing. Such light as the clouds did not stop, the trees did. There was nothing that Robert Collins could see, only the total blackness of the woods and the wind that he could not feel, and the weather making faster than even a duck hunter could want it.

There was a question here that did not occur to Robert Collins at the time, but which haunted him whenever he doubted what had happened at dawn. The question was, How he found his way back to the pond. In all the months that he roamed the Codifer Hills, he had not known that the pond was there. When he approached it the first time, he had been thinking ahead, of the ducks, and he had not been watching his way. He left it in total darkness, and in total darkness he found his way back. Later, in the middle of summer when the ducks are all in the north, this knowledge threatened his dream. But in the autumn, when the water fowl were pouring down the river on the blowing fronts and the island was once more like a dying sun, he felt certain that it was only because he did not know the way that he was able to find the pond again.

So sometime before dawn he was back at the pond, crouched against the logs, with the weather terribly cold. On such a morning the light does not even begin until the sun is well above the horizon, and then, in the first few minutes, it is even harder to see than on most nights. Ducks and geese, for unknown reasons, have to fly during this time. Robert Collins believed that they flew for the sheer, blind recklessness of burning through the searing cold of the air, of the noise and power in their wings, and of hurtling through space where they cannot see where they are going. But as he hid among the logs he was not thinking of that either. He found himself not thinking anything, only a dawning with the light of a supra-rational certainty that his gander was going to come.

And that time of light passed, and the ducks were there. The pond was empty, but the sky was full. The sky was full of orange daylight and noise and wind and wings and black, twisting, darting shapes. He rose among the logs, shot, missed, then powdered a hen teal crossing, got reloaded, and back-busted a wood-duck drake below the trees. Then he caught a greenhead mallard climbing straight above him. Collins fired, and the mallard missed a beat, wavered, leveled off, and missed another beat. He fired again, and the duck came falling, falling straight at him, getting bigger in his face, and landing with a whack in front of him. He pointed the gun up, picked up the duck, and spread its iridescent feathers in the light.

The ducks regrouped in high flocks, crossing and recrossing the open space above the pond. Robert Collins waded into the pond and picked up his ducks, stuffing them carefully into the pockets of his hunting coat, then climbed back up over the logs and hid among them to wait.

He waited for the ducks to settle back. At first they lit along the far edge of the pond, then fanned back toward him. Soon he was surrounded with feeding ducks. They filtered back in singles and pairs first. Then bigger flocks appeared, breaking up above the trees and ripping air as they settled into the open space. And then it seemed that all the ducks were back. They were quiet, feeding and chuckling softly on the pond. Inside his coat Robert Collins could feel the slain ducks still warm against his ribs. Together—the ducks, the trees, the pond, and he—they waited. And when they came, it was not suddenly. He knew when to look up, and he knew what he would see. They were there, all eighteen tiny crosses in a V formation against the sky. He waited while the geese passed once more overhead and out of sight, then waited until the geese came back. The geese were much bigger now, so that he could make out their long black necks. They passed back out of sight again, circled, and returned, making doleful goose talk that drifted sadly to him on the wind.

On the last pass, Robert Collins' focus became riveted on the gander. The gander passed overhead in a glide, then turning, banking, overawing in his sheer bigness, he set his wings for the last time and began sailing in, dead on at Robert Collins. Robert Collins was ready. The gander's wings were set like giant, slatted vanes, spread-eagled against the sky. Robert Collins had both hammers back. Then he was up from the logs, with the gun up. The heavy monstrous roar and recoil of the goose loads nearly knocked him over the dam, hitting the gander full and the feathers flying like smoke. But the gander kept coming, and Robert Collins got his balance, aimed, and shot again. The logs seemed now to disintegrate beneath his feet. The recoil sent him tumbling into the ditch, and he hit the mud, rolling at the foot of the dam.

Everything about him but his gun was covered with mud. The air above him was a pandemonium of escaping ducks. His lip was bloody, and a bruise was swelling above his eye. He breeched the gun and ejected the two spent shells. "Now it is over," he thought, and the wind got in below the trees and made freezing patches in his wet clothes.

He stood and peered out over the dam. The pond was empty, but for the goose. He lay inert, a gnarled, pitiful kind of spread eagle in the pond, with the water turning pinkish around him. Robert Collins climbed the dam and waded into the freezing pond. He picked up the goose, but did not hold it in the light. He held it in his own shadow, fingering the graying frazzle feathers around the gander's bill. The blood cast dissipated from the pond. Robert Collins turned away, looking at nothing. The wind was beginning to die.

The cold was setting in, deadly and solemn. Robert Collins started to leave.

Then a voice arrested him from somewhere back among the vines. He froze. It would be impossible for him to describe the revulsion with which that voice struck him. But it was as though all the filth of the land and the petty cowardice of its people were reaching out to reclaim him. "Hey, Buddy, ain't chu a little bit early ta be shootin' them boids?" Robert Collins did not turn to face the voice. He stood very still, slipping his hand into his pockets.

"How minney d'jou git?" said the voice. The voice seemed to think that it was all very amusing. But by then, Robert Collins was ready. At the same time that he turned, he slammed shut his breech so that as soon as he was facing the man, his gun was already up. Now the man froze.

"One too few," said Robert Collins.

The man made a slight move, as though to go for the revolver on his hip, but he hesitated and stopped with no gesture from Robert Collins. "You're under arrest," the man croaked, "in the name of the State Game and Fish Commission."

Robert Collins stared at the man, a short piggy-looking spectacle. He wore a green uniform with a shiny badge, and the leather of his holster creaked as he rocked nervously from one foot to the other.

Robert Collins pursed his lips. "At this range," he said, "it might take two shots and an hour for you to die. If you don't get hit in both eyes and blinded, you might be able to crawl back to town and find a doctor. If you do, I want you to tell them something for me. Tell them that I used to hate them, but that now they are less than insignificant to me." Robert Collins pulled the left trigger.

It was not loud after the two goose loads. Little red freckles came out all over the man's face. He put up his hands as he fell, and when he hit the ground, his hands fell away; his face was solid red.

Robert Collins walked up to the man and saw one eye still looking through the blood. He put the right barrel up against it and fired, gutting the man's head.

117

3

"I see," I said quietly. The pipe had gone out. I leaned over and emptied it by knocking it against my shoe. "Just one question."

He looked up suddenly. It seemed to occur to him that he had been talking to another person.

"How did you pray the ole man dead?" I said, handing him the pipe.

"Rotenone," he grinned. "Dumb nigger put it in his whiskey for me."

4

As it happened, Robert Collins and I and his blind mule made our way back and into Graceville in the rain. But it seemed that even in the rain itself there was indecision. It was neither the driving half-sleet of winter nor the warm Gulf rain bringing spring on a south wind. It started sometime before dawn in a dead calm, and it must have started slowly, because I didn't wake up until a big drop sifted down through the trees and hit me in the face. Robert Collins was already awake, sitting in exactly the position of the night before, staring at the fire and listening to the raindrops hiss when they struck the coals. I had to stop and think to remember that he had even gone to bed.

I raked my legs across some leaves to let him know that I was up, but he ignored it. I got up, sleepy, stiff and aching from the rough ground, staring at him for some sign of what we were going to do. He wasn't giving any. So I sat back down, wanting something to smoke. I spied the pipe lying on the ground between us, the pouch three feet from it on the other side of Robert Collins' feet. I wondered what to do. Finally I reached over and took them. Robert Collins seemed not to notice. So I loaded the pipe, lit it on a live ember, and leaned back against my tree to wait for the dawn or the dousing or whatever else was fixing to come.

The rain was slow at first, so we didn't get too wet. And before I finished the pipe, the false dawn began to grow among the trees. He still said nothing, still didn't move. It was only at some precise point in the progress of the growing day, when you suddenly realized that now you could see things instead of just the light, that he suddenly stood erect. "Well," he said, "let's get on with it."

He began moving immediately, quickly and efficiently gathering and packing everything that he had left around. He slung the outlandish 10-gauge across his shoulders and made for the mule, leaving me to follow as best I could. By the time I caught up, he had the mule loaded and untied. He gave me one glance, the meaning of which was not clear, then turned and began walking fast through the growing light and the increasing rain.

He set a superhuman pace. He knew where he was going, and I didn't; he knew the places that required careful footing. Once we got out of the dense bottom, the rain began hitting us full and hard. I couldn't see more than twenty feet in any direction, but Robert Collins walked with decision. I slid. I stumbled. I spread mud clear up my right leg and got stinging water in my eye. But I kept up. When I could, when I was walking erect, I kept my eyes on Robert Collins' back—I stared in wonder through the rain at his round, muscular shoulders.

So there was no one outside in the town when we came to the recognizable path that became what I had come to think of as the "main street" of Graceville. There was no perceptible change in Robert Collins' stride except that there was a change in the sound as his feet began falling on the relatively clear, puddle-covered path—the heavy *splat-splat-splat* in front of the aimless, crazy-legged shambling of the blind mule—but the sound made me look up and scan the open spaces in the town, and the wild thought came to me, "What is he leading me into? Do I want to just walk into this town like this?" And then, "Oh, my God! Where else could I go?"

He turned left, away from the jail, up the main street, and kept walking as though he didn't even remark the fact that he was in town. But I found myself looking frantically about. Searching—for what? Somebody waiting to shoot me? Some place to run and hide? My God! This man is a murderer.

But so are we, I guess, as far as they're concerned. Robert Collins kept walking.

We passed through the town without seeing a soul. Being in the rain was now more like standing in the rapids of a river than being in any mere shower of drops. As we neared the river, the main path turned, and we entered a portion that was out of sight of the rest. High up on a bluff, overlooking the river, was a white, two-story house with a screened-in porch, and away down to the right, on stilts above high water in the river, was a swamp cabin with lamp light in every window and what seemed to be a great deal of movement going on inside.

Although there was no light on in Collins' house, I could see an unrecognizable figure inside the screen porch. As we approached, he stood, pressed his hands and face against the screen, then let out a yell which neither Robert Collins nor anyone inside the lighted cabin seemed to hear.

"Who was he?" I thought. "Ole Beard's son!" My stomach went cold. I looked frantically about. For what? All I saw was rain.

As Robert Collins bore down on the steps, a gaunt, super-annuated Negro appeared through the door, taking the mule and leading it around behind the house, and then we were mounting the steps and the figure, which now appeared as a youth with a quarter-inch growth of never-shaven beard, stood aside and faced Robert Collins pointedly. "Hit's Ole Baird!" he said, before Robert Collins even stopped.

I wavered in the door, then finally stepped onto the porch and out of the rain.

The boy's stare wavered between Robert Collins, to whom it communicated a puerile outrage and demand for revenge, and me, with withering hatred.

"They killed him!" he screamed with tears filling his face.

Then Robert Collins fixed him in a cold, malevolent gaze, then turned and strode back into the house.

5

That night I had another nightmare. They were all chasing me—Arnold, Ernie, Collins, Ole Beard, Sorry, and a lot more of them —chasing me through the woods and the sticks and vines were hemming me in, and every time I would try to break one of them it would be my fingers or my arm or my leg that would break instead. When I woke up, it was just dawn. Ernie was snoring on the floor, a bottle of Arnold's brandy overturned and spilled near his hand. I got up and walked out onto the back stoop.

The rain had stopped again, and winter had gained the upper hand. It was another of those bright windy days when the sky is high and thin and tired-looking. I stepped down into the yard, and the wind hit me straight out of the north like a gigantic ice mallet. "Blow," I thought. "Blow me away. Blow me into the ground. I can't take this much longer. I swear to God, I can't."

I walked—nowhere, anywhere, just walking—toward the grave-yard. Ole Beard's mound of blood-red clay was already sinking around the edges. I kicked it, and it was hard as stone, packed by the rain. So many graves; too many for such a small town. Too many people dead. Pretty soon there'll be a grave with Arnold Weathermore on it—on it or in it? Fuck him. Oh, Jesus, I gotta get out of here. My God, there comes Robert Collins.

He was walking hard across the sodden leaves. I waved, over-gestured in the cold and surprise.

"What are you doing up?" he asked flatly.

"I had a nightmare. What about you?"

He stared at his feet and kept walking until only the wet mound was between us. "The same, I suppose." He kicked the mud. "Where's Ernie? He's supposed to be keeping an eye on you."

"Hung over."

"From what?" He looked up suddenly.

"Brandy. He got bombed last night."

"He what?" Then he looked away. "I need Ernie like I need a pet pachyderm." Then he stared indignantly at me. "I don't need any-body," he said. "And if I did, it wouldn't matter. They wouldn't be any good for me even if I needed them."

I wrinkled my brow. He was staring straight at me.

"Because people are asses, Dr. Fargus. People operate on the bas.s of a carrot hung in front of their nose."

"And?"

"That makes me very lonely." He looked back down.

I calculated. "What about your wife?" I said.

"What about her?"

"Where is she?" I ventured.

He shrugged.

"I take it she doesn't help either," I said. "Huh?"

He stared fixedly at me. "That's all right," he said. "That nigger'll get his soon enough."

"He will?"

"He will!" he shot back. "And—"

"What?"

"Nothing."

I looked away.

Then he said very quietly, "You're just like the rest of them, aren't you?"

"I'm not sure I'm qualified to decide that," I said.

"I just can't believe it," he said.

"What?"

"That I've been here this long, and gone through everything I've gone though, and now it's going to be destroyed because two idiots blundered in here on their way to a fishing trip.

"And not only that."

"What?" I said.

"That now it's going to be over"—he looked at me, shaking his head—"and nobody will even know that it ever was. Nobody will understand it when it's over."

"Understand what?" I said.

"The island," he said. "And the geese."

"The geese," I said.

Suddenly his face became rigid. The bones and muscles stood out as though he had no skin. "I don't know why I didn't blow your brains out while we were still in the woods," he spat.

"Oh—" I said. "Why didn't you?"

He gazed at me, and the rigidity melted. "I—" he said. "I'm going down on the bank and watch the ducks. This is probably the last cold of the year. In a week they'll be gone." He turned away, shoved his hands in his pockets, and started walking. I followed. We walked slowly down the last gradual slope to the river.

Behind us, the wind was whining among the grave markers. The cold was bitter. Collins walked rapidly, staring at the ground.

We emerged on a high bluff overlooking the fast muddy current. At this point the river narrowed, and the far bank was not over a quarter mile away. Along the far bank was a low, brown line of flooded button willows where ragged, wind-tattered lines and V's of waterfowl were lancing low across the water, calling faintly, desperately in the wind.

Robert Collins stared vacantly out across the hostile distance. I stood above him, looking at the back of his round head. "Listen—" I said.

"What?" he kept staring.

I said nothing.

One swift and vicious V of ducks shot across in front of us and disappeared upstream.

"Those," he said, "the ducks that just went past, those are canvasbacks. In a straight, level line, they're the fastest creatures on earth."

"Listen," I said.

"What?"

"I've got to get out of here," I said.

"Well, you won't," he said without looking up.

"What do you mean?"

"I mean I'll die for this. And I'll kill for it too. Until it's over and I can't do either anymore."

"What are you?" I said. "Some kind of a spoiled child? If I can't have my way, then nobody can? Is that it?"

"Maybe so," he said calmly. Then he looked up with a trace of a smile. "No, I don't think that's it. It's just that—even if I would like to let you go—it would be a sin. There wouldn't be any time to expiate for that sin."

"A sin against what?" I said.

"Myself"—he shrugged—"and—"

"What?"

"The geese." He smiled faintly and looked away.

I stared hard at his averted face. My breath was smoking hard, and my eyes were burning in the wind. "Well, why didn't you shoot me in the woods then?"

"Oh"—he looked back out across the water, then shook his head viciously hard for an instant—"because I was lonesome then, and

123

weak. I get that way sometimes. But now I'm not. And I won't let you go back and tell them where I am."

"Lonesome?" I offered.

"It's hard sometimes, Dr. Fargus."

"What's hard?"

"Seeing things. Feeling things. Fighting for things—when you know you're the only person in the world who sees them or feels them or cares about them. You know, I was sorry when I learned that it wasn't you who killed Beard."

"Why?"

He gave a deprecatory laugh. "Because then you'd have been a murderer like me. Killing for things, Fargus! Have you ever killed anybody?"

"No, I haven't."

"That's the hardest thing of all. Killing a person makes just lying down and dying look like a good night's sleep. It's hard to sleep after you kill somebody. It's hard to keep loving something when you have to kill for it."

"It? What is it?"

"The geese. The seasons. The island like the sun. Nothing you'd understand. Nothing anybody'd understand. I shouldn't have even tried to tell you. But that's what the loneliness will do to you. Anything that could make a person this lonely is bound to be inexpressible, but that's exactly what makes you have to rationalize it, or seduce somebody else to be in it with you." He shook his head and laughed drily. "The one thing that you do for no reason outside itself is the one thing you're most anxious to have somebody else understand. The one thing that you know you can't communicate is the one thing that you absolutely have to talk about."

"How do you know I don't understand, Collins?" I shot back at him.

"Because you can't," he said. "Because it's an in-principle impossibility for one man to understand another man's vision. And even if you did, it would take the meaning and the value out of my own suffering and loneliness."

"Right!" I said. "You're right. I can't understand that. I can't see what you see in an island—or a goose. But I've had visions too,

Collins. I've suffered. I've been lonely. I've wanted to talk about what seemed to me the most important thing in the world when I knew nobody else in the world wanted to listen to me."

He looked at me, and his face was very serious. "What was it?"

"Some research," I said. "Do you really want to hear about it?"

He almost smiled. "You could tell me what it was."

"Well—I had an idea for a way to cure vaginal yeast infections. I was going to call it the Fargus technique."

"Vaginal yeast infections?" he stared.

"At least, it's some good to somebody," I countered, "unlike killing a goose!"

"And that's where I'm one up on you," he said with a smile.

And I almost smiled back. "I guess it is."

He watched me for a long moment. Then his face became very sad. "Well," he said, "if you do understand as much as you claim to, then"—very slowly—"you have to understand that you would kill anyone before you'd let them stop you. . . ."

"Collins," I said, "I'm going to escape."

"I suppose," he said, "that you have to try."

I said nothing.

He continued, "And you understand that I have to kill you."

I stared at him, chewing my lip and saying nothing.

He turned and gazed vacantly at the river. "This right here," he said, "this is the hell."

I turned away from him and started walking as fast as I dared. I rushed up the slow slope away from the river and onto the main street of the town. As soon as I felt like I was out of his sight, I made for Ernie's door.

And as soon as I left Collins on the riverbank, I began to feel extremely cold. It seemed like the temperature dropped another twenty degrees between the river and Ernie's yard. By the time I got there, my insides were all knotted up. But just as I reached for Ernie's door, his voice bawled from inside the cabin so loud it stopped me in my tracks: "Laurie! Hey you goddam black wench."

"Whatchu want, white man?" I heard from the other cabin.

"Laurie!" Ernie bawled. "Get over here with that coffee!"

"Shet up," she called. "I'm comin' fast as I can."

Ernie grunted. I opened the door and stepped inside.

He was crouched by the tin stove trying to get it lit. He looked up at me and said nothing. His eyes were ringed with red, and his beard looked as if he had burned it in the stove. He looked miserable.

"Ah sweah ta Gawd"—Laurie burst in the door on a blast of wind, holding a blackened coffeepot—"Some men's ain't got no consid'ation for pore niggah's ole bones. Hit must be a hunnerd degrees cold out dah make me go runnin' roun' outside fetch yo' cawfy."

Ernie grunted.

" 'S'awright, dough, Lawd goan come take keer me an' leave you mek y'awn cawfy what you goan do then?" She wore an old woolen army coat that would have fit a two-hundred-pound man. She wiped her nose on the sleeve. "Wha' you want 'dis put?" she said to Ernie.

"Somep'm wrong wi' this wood stove," Ernie stared accusingly at her.

"What's dat? Oughta draw good today." She set the coffee on the floor.

"Can't get it lit," Ernie said. "Keeps goin' out."

"You ain't got de flue shet," she said, flipping the handle. "Ah sweah ta Gawd, you white mens is de helplessest critters on Gawd's green earth. Hyah, git outa my way." Her eighty pounds shoved giant Ernie aside. "Look ta me like ennybody know betta'n try ta sta't a fiah in dis kinda wind wi' de flue wide opem. You white mens is all alike."

She squatted like a bird before the stove door, struck a match, tended it for a second, then stood up. "Deah"—she pointed—"Mah Sorry, he ain't much, Lawd knows, but least he know bettah'n try build no fiah on a day like dis here wid de flue wide opem."

"Shoot," I said. "I bet he gets you so hot over there y'all heat up the whole house."

"Whatchu talkin' bout?"

"Just I bet one or the other of you gets to feeling cold and comes and huddles up to the other one and the other one gets to feeling

126

the first one rubbing up against him and pretty soon y'all both rubbing up against each other and first thing you know both of you so hot you bout to burn the bed up."

"You shet you mouf!"

"Cold mornin like this? With lots of snugglin'?"

She giggled and looked away.

"I know that's what I'd be doin'."

"You oughta be shamed," she said, but she was grinning. "I be 'long witchalls breakfast in a minnit"—and to Ernie—"You put some moah kindlin' on dah in a minnit an' don't opem dat flue till da smoke staht comin' out in de room." Then turning to the door, "I sweah ta Gawd, you white mens is all alike!" She left in another icy blast.

"Jeezus, it's cold," Ernie said. "What's got into you?"

"Not a thing," I said. "By the way, how's your foot?"

"What foot?"

"Where the chicken got you? I noticed you been walking around on it a lot."

"Yeah," he said, "I have." He stared hard at me. "And it's got perfec'ly all right."

"Oh, well," I stepped down to the fire and began warming my hands, "that's not the kind of doctor I am. I guess I just made a mistake."

"Oh, yeah?" He moved around and put a hand on my shoulder until I looked back up at him. "Then just what kind of a doctor are you?"

"A gynecologist," I said, looking away.

"A what?"

"A female doctor. I guess you'd call it a pussy plumber."

Out of the corner of my eye, I could see Ernie's jaw go slack. "A pussy what?"

"You know how you said your wife didn't like to fuck?"

"Yeah?"

"Well there's a whole lot of things that can cause that. My job is to try to help with some of 'em."

"No shit," Ernie said.

"That's right."

127

Ernie was leaning against the wall. Suddenly he jerked his head around toward the door. "I wish she'd hurry up wi' that food. My head's bout ta bust. These goddam niggers, I'm tellin' you!"

I stared at him for a second, thinking. "Here," I said. I went to the pack and got out a tin of aspirin. "Take about four of these," I handed them to Ernie. "Wash 'em down with a little of that coffee. Just a little though. Don't you know not to drink coffee when you've got a headache?"

Ernie stared askance at me. "What, you a headache doctor too?"

"No," I said, "but you don't have to be a headache doctor to know what to take for a hangover."

He stared at the aspirin.

"Where's the cups?" I asked.

He pointed to two dirty tin cans. I poured him about two swallows into one of them, poured the other one full for myself, then went to the door and poured out the rest of the coffee.

"Very bad for you to drink coffee with a hangover," I said.

He glared at the empty pot.

"Take those pills," I said.

He shrugged. He took them.

I sat down, set the pot in front of him, and sipped my coffee. "You know what you were saying about me being wrong about your foot?"

"Yeah?"

"Just think, though, if I hadn't of told you that we'd of never met," I said. "Not to talk or anything."

"I guess you're right," he said. He was staring at the fire. He reached over and opened the flue. There was a sudden, swift suction, and the fire reared up.

"Shit!" I said.

Ernie blinked. "What?"

"Here I am trying to play it cool," I said.

"Do what?" Ernie said.

"There's no point my playing cool with you, is there, Ernie?"

He stared for a second, then shook his head.

"Ernie," I said, chewing my lip, "you're a good man."

Ernie blinked.

128

"You're not smart. You're not citified. You're just a damn good guy."

Ernie wrinkled his brow and rolled his eyes down upon himself. "I don't see how I coulda made it this long without you."

"You're pretty good to talk to," he said.

"Thank you, Ernie."

He put a piece of stove wood on the fire.

"I just wanted you to know," I said, "that Robert Collins just told me he was going to kill me."

He froze. "That son of a bitch," he said. "He thinks he can just kill anybody he wants."

"I guess he can," I said. "Unless I can think of some way to keep him from it."

Ernie fixed his eyes on my face. He looked deeply troubled. "What you gonna do?" he said very slowly.

"I don't know. I'm thinking."

Ernie's eyes left my face and roamed the room. They paused on nothing except his shotgun.

"Ernie," I said. "Will you help me get out of here?"

"If I did," he said, "I'd hafta go on with you."

"I know."

"Where would I stay?"

"Nice place," I said.

"With you?"

"If you want."

He nodded. Then he got up and went and sat down on his cot. He was staring at the wall, away from me. He was chewing his lip and wringing his hands. I could see that he was breathing very hard.

I stared at the fire.

"Hey," he said.

I looked up.

He swallowed. He was staring out of the bottoms of his eyes, like the day before when he had been looking at Anna. "Do you think —outa all that pussy in your office—there might be some for me if I was to go?"

"Why do you think I brought it up?"

129

Ernie turned back to the wall.

Then the door burst open again. Laurie was in the room holding two plates of steaming eggs and grits. "Lawsamussy wassa matta you ain't got dat fiah lit rat yet. You white mens is *de mos'* hepless critters on Gawd's green earth!"

I looked at the fire; it looked fine to me.

She set the plates on the floor and rushed at Ernie, giving him a vicious shove off the cot and into the corner. "Gimme dat stove wood," she said, snatching a stick from the box and brandishing it over Ernie's head, "an' git on an' eat yo' breaffust fo' hit stonecol'." She stuck her head inside the stove and the barrage of abuse became incomprehensible.

Ernie was standing up now, staring at her.

"Ah sweah to Gawd," she said as she suddenly wheeled and stood up, "you white mens is all alike!" She darted for the door and slammed it behind her.

I looked at Ernie.

"Oh, hell," he said.

"What?"

"Now you got her goin'."

"What do you mean?"

"All that talkin' you done about her an' Sorry."

"What about it?"

"You give her a wide-on. She's goan be that way now for the rest of the day. And Sorry can't do a damn thing about it."

I shook my head and picked up my plate.

Ernie stood there for a long minute, then picked up his.

We held our plates, not looking at each other and picking at our food in silence.

Then, *blam-blam-blam!* Something was slamming against the door. I jumped and spilled scalding coffee on my leg. Ernie stood up and opened the door. Young Beard was on the steps, his face two feet below Ernie's, staring hatred at us both.

"You seen Mist Collins?" His voice was excited, and it cracked.

Ernie stared from him to me, then back to him. He faced Young Beard squarely. "No, I ain't," he said flatly.

Young Beard looked away from him and at me. "What's he doin' here?" he said.

130

Ernie said nothing. He drew himself up to his full height. He stared down at the boy. "Look, you little shit," he said very quietly, "you betta git yo' ass off my stoop rat now, and don't you nor none of yo' fambly evah come on my place again, you hear?"

The kid was shaking. He flushed with rage. Then he turned on me. "We goan git you," he said to me. "We goan hang you by the balls."

Then Ernie slammed the door in his face.

"Okay," he said, looking at me. "You tell me what to do, an' we'll git outa here."

So I told him about Arnold's idea of propping the pontoon up and fastening the airplane to a tree. I didn't even consider the other idea because it seemed too slow. He listened in silence, responding only with an occasional blink. All he said when I finished was, "Is that nigger comin' with us?"

"I don't know. If he can—if he will. If not, we'll go without him."

Then Ernie got up.

"Where are you going?" I said.

"I'm gonna take me a walk," he said, "one last look around."

And he was right, I thought. Now that we had said it, it was no time for us to be together. I thought about getting up and going outside too, but the wind was out there and Robert Collins sitting on the bank watching the ducks. I didn't want to run into Robert Collins now.

Ernie paused a long time in the door. I could feel him looking at me. Why didn't he hurry up and leave? Something was making my eyes water. Some kind of a nervous force was rising, pushing up through my back, forcing me down into the floor. I felt like I was passing out. Some endless time later I heard the door open and Ernie's stiff-legged footfall move onto the stoop. Then the door closed.

I stood up and looked shakily at the room. It was just a room, just a cabin, but it had real wood and metal and cloth in it, the real things of a room. I touched the iron frame of the cot, and it felt strangely, impressively alive.

"But Arnold said it was possible," I made myself say. Arnold said that was our only hope. Arnold!

They're going to hang Arnold. It ought to be me and Arnold, but they're going to hang Arnold. Why? Why all of this? It ought to be me and Arnold, and they're going to hang Arnold, and Arnold won't come, and they're going to shoot me and Ernie with 10-gauge buckshot and the dogs are going to eat us and I'm going to kill Ernie and then I'm going to crash the airplane into the trees because I haven't flown an airplane since 1945. And why? Because Arnold wants to have sex with an insane woman.

"And you'd better cut that out," I said aloud again.

Calm down—that's your only hope. I went over the pack, looking for liquor. Why hadn't he packed any Wild Turkey? That's what I'm gonna be when Robert Collins starts shooting, a biologically managed wild turkey. A dead duck? A screwed goose. Arnold plus Anna—touching!

Fargus minus one—nothing. Henry Fargus—pussy plumber. Henry plus Alice. I remembered Alice. Why did I remember Alice? Whiskey—not Wild Turkey—but whiskey! Yankees and niggers have no taste in either women or whiskey. I broke the seal and upended the bottle, gagged, swallowed, and repeated the whole performance. White Southerners have all the taste except that the women are just stupid.

I was fixing to get myself killed. The whiskey was roaring up in my ears. The Fargus technique was fixing to get myself killed.

Then I wanted my stupid southern woman. I had a flash of her and me under a palm tree on a beach somewhere, and I was drinking bourbon on the rocks and she was knitting, and some little kid with sand all stuck to him was walking toward us, saying, "Look, Granddaddy, a shell," and I wanted that. I wanted to be there. I wanted it in a way that I'd never wanted the Fargus technique. I wanted her harmless old wet menopause eyes and her insipid knitting and her bony hands with the encroaching psoriasis that were about as smart as monkey paws, but Robert Collins was going to shoot me in the back with buckshot, and his dogs were going to eat me before I died.

I drank, broke out coughing, and drank again. I staggered over to the cot and sat on it. "I want to live," I said aloud. I drank. Dear Lord, don't let me get killed. I just want Alice. "I just want Alice." But the dogs were going to eat me. "I want Alice." I drank again, and barely got the bottle set on the floor before I fell over on the bed.

I was crying. "I don't—I don't—I don't want to get eat by dogs!" Moiling and boiling all over me. "Alice!" Alice. alice

When I woke up, the sun was coming sideways into the west window. It was cold. Oh, God, was it ever cold where I had just been. The stove was out, but when I got up to fix it—to light it, that's what you do to a stove—my hands were shaking so badly I couldn't. Where—where in the hell did Ernie keep the matches? There, matches. Something about the flue. Close it to light. Wind, like some kind of cold vapor that took away more heat than mere air could ever carry, was rising up from the cracked floor and getting in around the door, rolling over me in waves. I reached for the flue; it wouldn't move. Frozen. I forced it shut, and it groaned like it was dying.

The sound stopped me. There was helplessness in the sound. I looked around the room. The windows were iced over on the inside. The sound went on and on inside my head, wailed like a lost and dying soul. There are times, especially when I have just waked up, especially when I drank myself to sleep—times when the things that I've done and, even more, the thing that I am seem insupportable. Myself, in the role of all the things I've ever done, dances around my head like a party of demons. I know that I am going to die. I knew it then. I was killing Ernie, and Robert Collins and Arnold, and the Fargus technique, rearing its head like Grendel, was going to break off my arm.

"So go on and do it," I said. I broke out coughing, coughed up bile and phlegm, and spat them out on the floor. My selves looked from me to where I had spat, then stared back at me out of the icy room. Icicles were hanging down along the edge of the roof. My throat was very sore. "So that's how it will be," I said. "I'll probably get out of this just fine, and then go back and die of pneumonia." That ought to be some kind of justice.

Oh, my God, but does it have to be so cold? I turned back to the heater. The wood was all stacked up beside it, the shavings for kindling, some shorter sticks, and then the big stove wood. I bunched

133

some of the shavings into a mound and struck a match to them. When they blazed, I stuck some of the sticks into the flame, and when they caught, I put two sticks of the stove wood on top. Smoke was pouring out into the room, so I opened the flue. It sucked viciously, and the blaze flared.

I put on two more of the big pieces. "Fargus the Boy Scout"— God, my throat was sore. My hands were warming over the fire. I was swallowing fire. "What the hell," I said, reaching for the bottle. What the hell? I swallowed more fire. Heat—pain, but heat. Sometimes pain is better than cold. Blaze, fire. I dashed some of the whiskey onto the fire and watched it flare and smelled the sickly sweet tinge it gave the smoke. Then I drank again.

The door burst open. Ernie stood there staring at me. "It's tonight," he said. He closed the door.

"What's tonight?"

"The hangin'."

"Whose?"

"That nigger's."

"They're not planning to get me too?"

"I don't know, but we got to go quick. How we gonna do this?"

I handed him the bottle. He took it, drank gratefully, then crouched and crowded me away from the fire.

"I'm depending on you," I said as he rubbed his hands together, "to get us back to that place where the airplane is. I'll explain the rest when we get there."

"We got to have guns," he said, his voice trembling from the cold or what I could not tell.

"Why?"

He shot me one look, then turned back to the fire.

"Well," I said, "you still have that revolver."

"There's the shotgun," he said, gesturing toward the door, "but there's no shells."

"Can't you steal some?"

He shrugged.

I reached for the bottle and took a small swallow, then looked back at him.

"It's cold," he said, suddenly speaking very softly.

I watched him as he glanced up at me and then back at the fire, still rubbing his hands together. "It's goddam cold," he said.

The late evening sun was slanting in through the ice. It was the kind of golden cold light that I remembered from when I was a little boy on sad Sunday afternoons late in the Christmas holidays when I knew that all the good days were over and tomorrow I would have to go back to school. "So," I said, "tomorrow we'll have steam heat." I handed him the bottle.

He looked contemptuously at it, took a heavy pull, and set it down hard behind him.

"Damn right, it's cold," I said, "and it's gonna be even colder when we're sloshin' around out in that lake. What we're doing is no game for chickens, but then we're not doing it for chicken shit either."

He said nothing. He seemed fascinated by the fire, the one tiny place of movement and heat in the frigid room. "Laurie build this?"

"I built it."

"She always builds my fire. Always raises hell about it too. Always tells me how goddam useless white men are cause they can't build their own fire."

I breathed heavily and hoped he didn't hear me.

"I'm hungry," he said.

"So eat."

"There's nothin' here."

"Why not?"

"It's all over at Laurie's."

"Call Laurie."

He looked at me and said nothing.

I picked up the bottle and read the label, then took a small sip. I looked at the label from the side, then pointed at the neck with a glance toward Ernie.

He reached for it and took another heavy swallow.

I stood up. "Where is Robert Collins?"

"Him and Young Beard down there fixin' up the scaffold."

"Where does he keep the shotgun shells? I'm gonna go steal some." Then I added, "the buckshot."

135

"You'd never get around his nigger."

"We need a chain too, a big heavy chain with a piece of iron that'll stick through the links."

"How we goan around in that froze water?"

"What do you mean, How? We're just gonna do it. Aren't you a goose hunter? Don't goose hunters have to walk around in freezing water?"

"No, I ain't a goose hunter. I ain't no kind of hunter except a meat hunter. And that just when I hafta be. Mist Collins is a goose hunter. Mist Collins walks in freezing water. Mist Collins can shoot a goose's head off at ninety yards with a rifle—flyin'!"

"Not if he doesn't catch us."

"He's gonna catch us," Ernie said. "An he's gonna shoot your head off, and then he's gonna tell me to turn around and get my ass back where I belong an' where I been all my life. An' you know what? I'm gonna go."

"Cause he's right?"

"Cause I'm scared!"

"Oh, I see. He doesn't walk in freezing water, he walks on it."

"What you mean?"

"Like Jesus. Robert Collins is Jesus or something."

"What kinda talk is that? Is that big city talk? Is that the way they talk where you come from?"

"Not all the time."

"I don't like that kinda talk."

"What kind?"

"Jesus-cussin'. Fuck and goddam is all right, but I don't like Jesus-cussin'."

"Well, you won't have to be around people that Jesus-cuss."

"Well, don't talk that way."

"All right. You've got me over a barrel. How do you want me to talk?"

"I don't know."

I said nothing. He said nothing.

"We need a chain," I said.

"Don't talk about that either," he said. "Nor the froze water."

"What do you want me to talk about?"

136

He stared at the fire and pretended to warm his hands—mine were warm, and I was farther from it than he was. "Tell me about the girls again," he said deliberately. "An' about what kinda place I'm gonna get me to live in." He rubbed his hands slowly together. "A warm place—nice—where the heat comes in in pipes." He turned to me. "They have them, don't they? Cause I remember they did when I was in Baton Rouge."

"Sure," I said.

"And the girls."

"Yes?"

"All young, huh?"

"I'll see that you don't get any other kind."

"Do you think they'll like me?"

"I'm sure most will."

"But they won't want to marry me."

"No. Most of them are already happily married."

Then he looked up at me and smiled. "You know, I didn' know they had that in the city. Guys to test out women."

My stomach turned over. "I think you'll be surprised at a lot of things they have in the city."

"If we make it." He smiled.

"If we make it." I slapped him on the shoulder.

"Come here," he said, getting up. He walked across the room, and I followed. He slid the bed out from the wall, and under it was a loose board which he pried up with the nail that was standing upright in its hole. Underneath were maybe a hundred rounds of 10-gauge ammunition. "I been plannin' this a long time," he said. "Ever since my wife died, I been thinkin' I might as well to leave. But, goddamn, I never thought it'd be like this."

I fixed his eyes with mine and gave him a nod.

He nodded back, then began scooping shells into a cloth bag.

"We've still got to have a chain," I said.

"I can get one," he said.

"Can you get it alone?"

"Why?"

"Because there's still one more thing I've got to do."

"That nigger?" he said.

137

"Listen," I said. "He's one grand helluva lot better pilot than I am. He's worth most anything it takes for us to spring him and get him to fly that plane for us."

"Okay," he said. "You know, and I don't."

"You get the chain and meet me back here," I said. "As soon as we get back, we'll be ready to go."

He stood up, dropped the last shell into the bag, and watched me go out the door.

Outside it was even colder than before, but the wind had stopped and the whiskey was warm inside me. The sun was setting quickly with a deep remote light through the trees. I walked slowly, reasonably carefully, skirting the town and moving through the high weeds that grew between the cleared area and the woods. The two-thirds full bottle was sloshing in my back pocket. I didn't think anybody could see me from the town. Besides, when it's this cold you don't pay much attention to anything besides your own feelings and the business strictly at hand, which was, for them, hanging Arnold. And maybe me! I never had figured out when they intended to come after me. I wondered if Robert Collins intended to do that himself, if he was just letting Young Beard help with Arnold to shut the kid up—but somehow, that didn't seem like Collins' style. For some reason I felt he would want to come after me on his own. Or maybe he just took it for granted that he could get me whenever he wanted.

They took a lot for granted around this place, if you asked me. Now what was that supposed to mean? Your brain's getting frozen, I mouthed to myself. So what? myself mouthed back. I can think anything I want as long as I don't get scared again. And if I get scared, I've got the bottle. It doesn't matter what I think or what I have to do. There's no rules except to get that airplane in the air. No rules except to get the pontoon propped up that's probably iced under by now, to get the engine cranked that's been out in this weather for how many days, to get the thing out of that lake when I haven't flown an airplane since 1945, all without Collins blowing our brains out. And Ernie, poor Ernie, what was he going to think the second he realized that you can't hold onto the struts of a flying airplane long enough to climb inside the cabin? Because I didn't know how Arnold had that part figured, but I didn't see how it could be done. Ernie! Oh, God. I reached for the bottle and took a long pull.

The weeds were board-stiff. I kicked a cluster of broom sedge. It budged, bent sickly somewhere deep in the earth. The sun was going down; the sky was deepening. I walked. I walked. The cold suddenly made it all seem pitifully insignificant. The cold was everywhere. It filled everything. The giant, blackening air bore down on the woods like a glacier, a black glacier. What was anything when the whole sky could get that cold? What was Robert Collins and his geese? What was me and that airplane? I had the image of a mosquito trying to fly out from under a boot. I wished I had some boots. My hands were stiff, even deep in my pockets. My legs were stiff clear up to my knees. I walked.

Up at the top end of the town was a big red glow, about the size of a house. I walked more carefully. I crouched below the tops of the broom sedge. I could see the black shape of the top half of the jail, and then the flames licking up into the trees not far from it. My stomach quailed, for no particular reason that I could think of. I began to pick the place that I would put down each foot. I took giant silent steps. I skirted the end of the town, and came out in the high weeds just above the jail.

The woods and sky were dark. Collins and Young Beard had a huge bonfire going about sixty feet from the jail. They moved around it like wraiths, carrying timbers and hammers, their breath steaming in the light. The flames rolled and roared, and the smoke seemed intensely white. They did not speak. They seemed to be finished with whatever they were doing because they were throwing all the wood onto the fire. The fire consumed it and crackled with relish. The flames rose in giant balls. Time and again it looked like they were standing in it and I couldn't see why it didn't take them too. Finally they just stood there, black against the red light. The jail was a massive solid shape against the dark transparency of the sky. The water in the logs would be frozen. It would be stronger and heavier than solid iron. The scaffold was somewhere out in the darkness; I couldn't see it.

I crouched in the grass trying to think what I could do. It's easy to see what's going on in a lighted area when you're standing in the dark, but almost impossible to see out of a lighted area into a dark one—at least I hoped that was the way it was. Anyhow that would mean that with Collins and Young Beard standing by the fire I could move around to the jail in the dark. If I didn't make any noise . . . , if I was lucky. The hell with it. I moved.

I belly-crawled across the cleared place around the building and came up behind it, wondering if I could afford to risk going around in front to use the door. Then I caught a gleam from a chink in the logs. I made for the chink, but it was too small. All I could see through it was light; there was a light on inside the jail. Did that mean somebody was in there? I took off crawling, looking for my bigger chink where I'd watched Ernie and the chicken.

But nothing felt the same in the cold. The log wall felt like the scaly back of some awful monster. I couldn't find the hole. Arnold, for God's sake, where's the hole? If I crawl any farther, they're gonna see me. There was no sound in the cold. Nothing except the scrub of my knees on the frozen ground. Then off in the woods a branch crashed. Who was coming? Where? I flattened out on the ground.

Then I saw the chink, but there was almost no light coming through it. Of course—it was on the other side of the room. I forced calm, then planted my eye in front of the chink.

The first thing I saw was Arnold. They had him chained by his feet to the bars, but the cell door was wide open.

And his face was as black as any nigger I ever saw. He was lying on the crown of his head with his face tilted backward. His mouth was open, and his eyes were closed, and he was breathing slowly and very heavily. His hands lay open at his sides. He looked like he was meditating, concentrating, preparing himself for something—For what?

Then Anna moved into view. Naked. I saw then why she wore dresses clear to her feet and long sleeves. Her skin below the neck was crossed and crisscrossed with scars and stripes so profuse that it looked like a reptile's. Her body was thin, gaunt, almost withered, but very hard-looking at the place where the withering stopped. Her hair was snarled and knotted, matted with briars.

She walked into the cell and knelt in the triangle that Arnold's spread legs formed with the bars. She seemed entranced. When she began, her ministries to him were almost ritualistic. Arnold did not open his eyes. He sucked in his cheeks, and once I heard the breath escape between his teeth. The only other sound they made was later—a scream. I don't know what it looked like because I turned away.

I don't know how long I lay there, but sometime later I heard a sound at the front door. When I looked up at the chink, there was no light inside the cell at all.

"Arnold!" I hissed.

Another limb crashed somewhere in the woods.

"Arnold!" I hissed louder.

"Hey, man, is that you?"

"Yes," I breathed. "Thank God it was just the wind."

"What you talkin' bout?"

"Are you alone?"

"Like the highest star! Like the deepest fish! Like the blackest nigger in Africa, I am alone."

I hesitated, then scrabbled around and up into the door. Inside there was no light whatsoever. I crouched in the doorway, waiting for my eyes to adjust, for something to come into relief against the black. Nothing appeared. "Arnold," I whispered, "can you see?"

"More than this darkness can conceal," he said.

"Have you got a match?"

Suddenly there was a flare in the cell, faster than I was prepared to see it come. He held the match to his face and grinned. And he was blacker than the surrounding walls, blacker than the darkness itself around that grin. His eyes were sunken. His jaws were slightly caved in. His mouth was bearded with a sort of greenish tinge about the hairs.

"Arnold," I said. "Are you all right?"

"He-he-he-he, ha-ha-ha! All right? All right! So the free world's come to see the poor nigger that's about to get hanged. He-he-he-he!"

"Arnold, listen to me. Goddamm it, cut that out." I ran toward him, and as soon as I did so, he blew out the match. I stumbled against the desk and went down with a sharp pain, like a broken bone, in my shin. But the bone wasn't broken. Don't be paranoid. I groped my way up in the dark, and Arnold struck another match.

"Sheeeit," he said grinning. "You know that thing was burnin' my fingers."

"Arnold," I said, holding onto the desk, "you're not gonna get hung."

"He-he-he!"

"Listen," I said. "We gotta get outa here. We gotta bust outa here. You're not gonna get hanged, but you gotta listen to me. We gotta do something."

He was grinning, sitting up and holding the bars. Then he reached out and shoved the door. It vibrated open with a grating squeak.

"My god!"

"He-he-he-he, ha-ha-ha." He reached into his pocket and produced a key which he waved, still grinning, before the light.

"Well that's great!" I said, but he blew out the match and I had to wait until he found and struck another. "That's great. Now look, what—"

"That's nothin', white man."

"What do you mean? Where'd you get that key?"

"She gave it to me."

"Who gave it to you?"

"Aw, what is that little piece of white snatch's name?"

"You mean that woman—Anna?"

"Yeah, that's the one. He-he, ha-ha."

"Arnold, what's wrong with you? We've got to get out of here."

"You've gotta get outa here. I ain't goin' nowhere, man. I'm goin' somewhere I won't never need to come back from. You tell 'em, hear? You tell 'em how it was: 'Arnold Weathermore, B.S., M.D., H.W.N., was hanged last night by the white establishment, but not before he had cuckolded its dictator.' "

"H.W.N.?"

"Half-White Nigger."

I said nothing.

"He-he-he, ha-ha!"

"Arnold?"

"White man! White man!"

142

"Look, dammit, you're not cuckolding anybody. Don't you know she's done that with every man Robert Collins ever hanged?"

Then his grin changed suddenly into a sneer. "Get out of here, white man."

"Arnold, listen—"

He waved the match wildly through the air, and the light spun nauseatingly between us. He reached out and snatched the door, slamming it in my face, and then the light was out, and I heard something tinkling across the floor and out the door into the darkness—the key. The room was solid with darkness. The only sound was the rattling bars, Arnold standing up, quaking wildly against them.

So I turned to leave. I walked to the door, opened it, and then Arnold screamed. It was no word. Just a scream that reverberated off the frozen logs.

I wheeled on him. "Well, would you for God's sake shut up so I can get away?" I hissed.

"It's death, Fargus," he said.

"Not for me if you'll just shut up."

"That's who I'm cuckolding, Fargus. He-he-he-he, ha-ha-ha. I'm cuckolding death.

"My ole man," he said. "He-he-he, ha-ha. His real problem wasn't that he was a nigger at all. It was that he let it kill him. And it's killing me too, but I've beat it, can't you see?"

"Sure, Arnold."

"White shit!" he screamed again, louder than before.

I stood there until the ringing died, then opened the door, stepped out, and ran head on into Robert Collins. I bounced back a foot and stood there staring at him.

He stared back at me.

Young Beard appeared over his shoulder. "Git him too," he said. "Ernie too. Ernie's s'pose ta be watchin' him."

"Look out, Hank!" Arnold yelled. "He-he-he-he!"

They turned toward Arnold.

I broke and ran. I made it to the edge of the clearing, to the edge of the weeds, in the woods, before something hit me in the kidneys and sent me spinning into a thicket of frozen vines. When I came

143

up, Young Beard had me in a hammerlock about to break my arm.

He dragged me out of the woods, back across the weeds and back into the clearing, and finally stood me up in front of Robert Collins. "Wail watta you wanna do with 'im then?"

"Get that bottle of whiskey away from him," Collins said, "before he plants it between your eyes. Then handcuff him to that tree. We'll get him as soon as we finish with this one."

He went into the jail, then reappeared with another set of handcuffs just like the ones they had on Arnold's legs. Young Beard dragged me to the tree and held my hands behind me. Collins snapped them on.

Then they stomped into the jail. There was a noise; then they came out with Arnold. Each of them had a hammerlock on one of his arms. They dragged him past me, and he shot me a piano-key grin that caught the firelight in the middle of his black face. Then they jerked him around and disappeared with him into the darkness.

I leaned back against the tree and stared up at where the firelight played among its branches. For a second I entertained a notion of trying to shinny up it backwards and slip myself free over the top. But that was idiotic! Too goddamned high! Then I screamed—before I even knew I was going to do it—and it sounded just like Arnold had. I jerked and bucked against the chain—nothing. I slumped against the tree.

Then the three of them reappeared in the firelight at the top of the scaffold. *"White shit!"* Arnold bellowed again.

Collins slugged him in the face.

"I'm beating it, Fargus," Arnold yelled, but this time, instead of hitting him, Collins slipped the noose around his neck. Then they stood there in the firelight at the top of the scaffold, Arnold as black as the night between the two white men. "He-he-he-he, ha—" He stopped in mid-laugh, and the rope thwacked taut.

I sat there staring. Arnold was out of sight, out of the light. Young Beard leaned over and spat downward where he had fallen. Then they turned and started descending, disappearing heads last down the ladder.

I jerked against the chain, jerked again, and felt it cutting into my hands. They were coming. They had disappeared because they were coming after me. Where were they? I couldn't see them. How far was it from there to here? I jerked again, and then somebody grabbed me from behind. I turned and saw the hand—Ernie's—and he had the key.

6

We were just coming in sight of the lake when the first hound bawled. I stopped running. "They catch on fast," I said, the cold air searing my lungs.

Ernie was behind me. He passed me, making no response, bulling through the frozen weeds with his fantastic, stiff-kneed, step-heave-wheeze, step-heave-wheeze, his cheeks puffed, the hundred pounds of rusty chain wrapped clinking around his shoulders. He ignored everything. He was, I realized, moving as fast as he could. His close-set eyes seemed fixed straight ahead, staring at something I couldn't see, some vision in the lake. The dog bugled, and I started jogging again.

The ground was stone-hard. Ernie had said that was good; the dogs wouldn't be able to smell. But what if the lake was frozen? My lungs were frozen—or on fire. I wanted to stop running. God, how would we have enough strength to do everything we had to do to the plane after running like this? Quit thinking! "Ernie," I said, drawing alongside him—the dog bawled again—"did you load the guns?"

"They loaded." He did not break rhythm.

I stopped again and looked back into the darkness where we had been. I wondered if I could hit anything with that pistol. I couldn't even see anything. The darkness seemed like it would help their shooting and hurt mine. I had the feeling that Robert Collins owned the darkness and could fill it with lead anytime he wanted. I started running again. Up ahead was the lake in starlight, but it didn't seem to be getting any closer. I concentrated on the running, on breathing. I tried breathing through my teeth. It helped my lungs, but it hurt my teeth. My side was beginning to catch. I hoped to God my side wouldn't start hurting. If it did, I wouldn't be able to run anymore. I could feel the twinge though. I could feel it turning my jog into a stumbling sort of gallop. I put on more speed.

Then I tripped. One second I was running; the next, I was footloose in black space; and the next, I hit the ground. Nothing I hit gave. I slid across the frozen ground like it was made of glass. For a second I was stunned; I couldn't believe it. Where was I, lying on the ground like this? I lay still while the heave-step-wheeze went past. It went away and stopped. There was no sound. Then a hound squalled, and I realized that I was out in the goddam jungle miles away from home in Jackson where nobody cared whether I lived or died, where the ground jumped up and hit me in the face, and it was so goddam dark you couldn't see it coming, and there was a bunch of men with dogs running around with guns trying to kill me, and then I was boiling mad, and I didn't care how cold it was, because I was Dr. Henry Fargus and I wasn't hurting anybody; I was just trying to help people and do a good thing, so I didn't deserve to die, and so I was half-up skidding sideways again down the frozen bank with the gun out, looking for something to shoot, and there wasn't anything except the night, anywhere. I stopped, breathing. The gun was shaking wildly in my hand. Except for me, the night was dead silent. The shaking wasn't from the cold. I might be passing out, but I was warm. I could feel the sweat on my face. I put the gun back in my pocket and touched my face. It wasn't sweat. Blood. I wished the dog would howl again. I wished it would run at me so I could kill it. I wished they'd all come so I could kill them all. There was no sound. I picked my way back up the frozen slope and started following Ernie.

When I caught up with him, he was sitting at the edge of the lake with the chain coiled in front of him and the shotgun laid across the chain, breathing in long quivering sobs. I stepped and caught a low branch. I hung there, breathing above him. There was ice all around the edge of the lake, but I could see the water rippling about the plane. The plane looked good from here—but what could you tell? I stopped myself from thinking that. I wanted to get to work. My lungs were screaming, but I wanted to get to work. I wanted to do it all myself. I wanted to shoot Ernie and prize the pontoon up all by myself and then take off and bomb this island

146

out of existence. I felt like I was forcing flames up my trachea every time I breathed.

Then a hound squalled long and loud, and then another joined it, and another. I scooped up the shotgun and stared at Ernie.

"That last 'ern's a smart dog," he said, staring up at me. "If she knows what she's lookin' for, we in trouble."

I wanted to shoot him. "How can you tell?" I hissed.

"I lissened to them dogs all their lives. That last 'ern, you don't fool her."

"What do you mean, If she knows what she's lookin' for?"

"Can't tell," he said distantly. "Might be a deer."

"Well, let's get to work."

"You tell me!" he said. "You got to tell me what to do."

"All right. All right. How will you know if they're really on our trail?"

"Hafta hear em again. See if they're gettin' closer." He was breathing heavily again, staring at the lake. "It won't be no problem tellin' if they're really after us."

"Okay," I said. "Look, here's what we've gotta do. That left pontoon is sunk. It's got a big gash in it, and it's at least partway full of water. Now what we gotta do is get a long log and a short log, and go out there and lift that pontoon and prop it up to where it's even with the one that's floating."

"Whatta we need with this chain then?"

"That's for later. Let's do one thing at a time."

"Okay," he said. "Okay, let's go."

He started for the lake, and I followed. He stepped on the thin sheet ice that ringed the open water, and it moaned and cracked with a teeth-edging sound. I stepped into the open water of his wake. The water didn't shock me immediately. It crept inside my shoes and canvas pants like slipping death, following fantastic patterns around my feet and ankles until they were soaked and completely numb. Ernie was crashing through the ice, breaking it open in front of me, and the little pieces were floating up in my path, glinting in the starlight and brushing against my legs, but I couldn't feel them because in less than ten seconds and without any warning my legs had no feeling at all.

A dog—two, three, more—bawled in the distance. Ernie? They were chorusing. Ernie, how smart are those dogs? Where's the shotgun? Back there with the chain. I could keep us covered while Ernie was working. Maybe I would do that after I got Ernie started. I wanted to check the electricity in the plane, but I might do that when I finished if it was going to take Ernie very long. He should have brought the shotgun. I'd go back and get it as soon as I'd checked the electricity.

Ernie bulled through the ice like a wounded animal. He stomped it and kicked it. It was bound to be tearing his legs. I wondered if he could feel it. Once he fell, and the water went over his waist. He never said a word.

Then we were in the open water. The dogs were chorusing, getting nearer. Ernie reached the plane first and stood under the wing, staring at it in awe. The starlight glinted on the silver wings. The prop stood black and motionless.

I slogged up beside him and pulled up onto the struts. "Okay," I said. "You see that pontoon? That's what we got to prop up. You go get some logs. I got to check something inside here."

He looked at me stupidly. "Get some logs!" I said.

"That thing's too big," he said. "We can't lift that thing."

"It ain't heavy," I said. "It's big, but it's light."

He stared at me, pain in his face.

"Just get the logs," I hissed. "Can't you hear those dogs?"

He said nothing.

I forced the frozen doorhandle and swung up inside the cockpit. It was black dark inside; I couldn't see anything. I looked back out the window; Ernie had disappeared in the darkness.

I had some matches in my pocket. I struck one, held my hand around the flame, and tried to see how the thing worked. I found the ammeter and the switch. The match went out. I lit another. I flipped the switch. The control lights came on. The battery was weak but not dead. I still had no idea if it would crank the plane. I flipped the switch off and swung out the other door onto the floating pontoon.

There was no sound except the dogs. Ernie was nowhere in sight. I reached up and caught the huge, cold, black blade of the prop. I pulled, and it moved; it turned. I swung back inside the cabin and choked the motor, then climbed back down on the float and turned the prop around once, half again, then once again. There wouldn't be any chance of starting the motor by hand because there was no place to stand, but I wanted to make sure it was well primed. Well primed, but I didn't want to flood it. Where was Ernie? "Ernie!" There was no answer except a huge splash, as though a log were being thrown in the water. "Just wanted to know where you were," I said.

Then along with the dogs, I could hear something moving toward me through the water. I hung onto the pontoon, out of the water, staring in the direction of the sound. There was nothing to do now except to wait for Ernie. I wanted the shotgun and the chain. I wanted everything right here, now. I didn't like to think of what we needed being back there on the bank. I didn't want to get back into the nasty freezing water again. Ernie came up dragging a downed oak sapling about six inches thick. "Didn' even hafta chop," he said. "Musta blew down."

"Good, but we need another one—a fulcrum."

"A what?"

"Something to put under it so we can lift."

He said nothing, dropped the sapling, and turned back toward the bank.

"Ernie," I said. He turned. "I'm going back for the shotgun and the chain."

He shrugged and turned back into the darkness. I stared at the water, then jumped in. And I couldn't feel it. There was no difference, no feeling at all. I was glad. I didn't want to feel. I didn't want to feel anything ever again.

That was wrong. I did want to feel, but what I wanted to feel was so far away. And I didn't want to feel anything until I felt that. I moved. I worked. I had a job to do, and it didn't matter now whether or not I got it done, just as long as I kept doing it. I was moving through icy water. I was going to get the chain and the shotgun so I could shoot any man or dog that got in the way of the job I was doing. Now, if I could just keep from thinking.

The way wasn't hard to find once I found the broken place in the ice. The chain and the shotgun were right where it led to the bank. I followed the corridor through the ice until I walked out on the land. Once again, there was no difference. I picked them up. The chain was frozen to the ground, and the shotgun was frozen onto the chain, so I had to rip them up. I swung the chain over my right shoulder and let it hang down my left side. I checked the shotgun to make sure it was loaded. It was, but Ernie had the rest of the shells. The dogs were bawling closer and closer. But that was all right. I would shoot them when they got close enough. I didn't care.

I started back out for the airplane. Ernie was already at work on the pontoon. The ice skim was growing from the edges toward the center. I slogged up beside him, put the shotgun in the cabin, and set the chain down on the floating pontoon. "I can't move it," Ernie said.

"Have you got the pole under the pontoon?"

"Yes, it's just too heavy." He had about a three-foot stump under the pole.

"Is it slipping?"

"No. I just can't move it."

"Well, it's not the plane," I said. "It's the water in that pontoon."

"That ain't gettin' it up," he said.

"Well, lemme try to help. Have you got anything to put under it if we get it up?"

He kicked another stump, floating behind him. "Look," he said, "why don't you get over on that other side and try and over-balance it instead?"

"Okay, good idea." The dogs were coming closer, but I didn't say anything. I went around to the other wing and climbed up in the struts. "Okay," I said, "heave!" and I flung my weight as hard as I could toward the outside. I felt the airplane move.

"It's movin'," Ernie said, "but you got to get further out."

"Okay, just a second." I reached inside and picked up the shotgun. Then I picked up the chain. I heaved the chain up on top of the wing for more weight. Then I climbed up with it. I began inching my way out along the frosted wing. I could feel the airplane tilting under me.

"Hey," Ernie yelled, "it's movin'."

"Okay," I said, "just hang on. I can still go some more." The dogs were ungodly loud. The plane was moving under me.

150

"Hold it!" Ernie yelled. "The water's runnin' out of the float. Get ready to come back this away, or you'll flop it over on that side." I shoved the chain back toward the fuselage. "Okay, hold it. I'm fixin' to prop it."

"Make sure you prop it so that the float'll slide off."

"Okay, goddam it."

I could hear the thrashing in the water.

"Okay," he said. "Get down."

For a second I didn't move. My breath was quivering; I couldn't get it under control. There was sweat under my arms. "Come get this chain," I said. "I don't want to drop it in and lose it."

Ernie splashed around until he was under the wing. I handed him the chain, but kept the shotgun. I climbed down. Ernie was standing motionless beside me when I stepped back into the water. The chain was tangled around his arms.

"What now?" he said very softly.

"We got to chain it to something good and solid."

"And then it'll be over?"

"Just about."

"Cause I'm cold."

I said nothing.

"I ain't never been this cold in my whole life."

"Neither have I," I said flatly.

"My feet"—his jaws worked a moment without sound—"my feet."

"I know," I said, "mine too. But there's not much more, and we gotta get it done quick cause those dogs are damn close."

He said nothing.

"Look," I said, pointing to a cross brace in the pontoon struts, "have you got the bolt?"

He nodded.

"Well, take the chain on back there and hook one end around something solid. Then we got to hook it around that thing, but don't do it yet because I got to show you just how to do it. Just wrap it around there so you don't get the chain too far back so it won't be long enough."

He blinked stupidly at me.

"Here," I said, "gimme one end of the chain." He didn't move,

151

and I took one end of the chain and wrapped it around the strut. "Okay, now go hook the other end to something solid as hell."

"Okay," he said, "okay. I will." He looked at the chain. "Cause I don't give a shit no way. Cause it ain't true, is it? I mean about you needin' somebody to test pussy and all. Just so we nearly through."

"What're you talking about?"

"Nothing," he said, "I don't give a shit. But—" He looked at me now. "But I just wannid you t'know I'd of helped you out anyway. I knew that the first day we talked. Cause we talked good. I hadn' talked so good since I was a kid."

"Whaddayou mean?"

"I mean it don't matter about the pussy and all. Just tell me how it would have been one more time."

"What would have?"

"You and me workin' together all the time, ever' day. Where we could talk ever' day. And plenty of booze?"

"Right, right! Now if you'll just go hook up that chain where we can get out of here before those dogs eat us alive."

"Okay," he said slowly. "Just so it's over quick. Cause I ain't never been so cold in my whole life."

I said nothing. He turned and began slogging away in the darkness, paying out the clanking, splashing chain behind him. He disappeared into the dark. The dogs felt like they were going on inside my head. I gripped the shotgun like grim death. The dogs cut loose all at once; it sounded as if they were right over my head. I turned in the water. Ernie was splashing behind the airplane. I could see the vague shapes of movement on the bank. The shotgun was up and roaring out a gigantic fireball across the frozen black lake. The dogs bawled. Somewhere in the woods I heard a shout. The shotgun blazed again in my hands. The dogs were going mad. "Ernie, for God's sake, hurry up!" God damn him! God damn him! I broke the shotgun and realized that Ernie had the rest of the shells, so I dug in my pocket for the revolver. I got it out and waved it in the black space, but there was just noise, and I didn't shoot. I could hear Ernie grunting and the chain clanking and splashing, and then another shout in the woods. I wished to God I had the rest of the shotgun shells. I wanted to kill somebody. Ernie, for God's sake hurry up. I'll buy you a whole whorehouse if you'll just hurry up.

"Ernie, goddam it, they're coming!" The chain jerked three times, very hard, and then came taut. I was sobbing out loud, and the tears were freezing on my cheeks. I fired the revolver at a movement on the bank, and someone shouted again in the woods. Then Ernie was wallowing back toward me. "Gimme some shotgun shells!" I said. "They're right there on the bank."

"It's just dogs," he said. "Le's go. Le's get outa here." He handed me two shells. I loaded the gun as he stood shivering beside me. Then I showed him how to pin the chain with the bolt.

"Look," I said. "You got to make sure both links are close together and both right at the bottom of the bolt so it'll all let go at once. If it don't, we're screwed."

"Okay. What are you gonna do?"

"I'm gonna get inside and try to crank the motor. Now you stand here on the good float and hold the pin. You keep holding it until I race the motor real fast and then"—my mouth gaped soundlessly—"and then when I race it real hard and hold it there, you hang on real tight and let go of the pin. Then," I said, and my mouth gaped again, "then you climb inside as fast as you can."

He stared at me for a long second while the dogs howled. "Okay," he said, and I moved.

I climbed up on the float and swung up into the cabin. I looked back just once to see Ernie squatting on the back end of the float, holding up the pin just like I told him. Then I slammed the door on everything. I held my breath. I pushed the starter. It made a noise, faltered, and stopped. I could hear the dogs and shouting even inside the cabin. I pushed the starter again. It turned over once, twice, three times. The motor coughed, sputtered, backfired. Everything stopped. I hit the starter viciously. The prop spun. The motor caught, sputtered, coughed, sputtered again, then roared. I let it run at half throttle, yelling, "Not yet, Ernie, not yet!" I turned on all the lights and lit up all the stumps ahead. The wind was all wrong, but it wasn't hard. The generator needle was charging away over to the right, and the lights were very strong. I reached for the throttle and shoved it wide. The engine raged. The whole plane was straining. "Okay!" I yelled. "Okay! Okay! Let go!"

Then something gave. The airplane bucked forward and paused. There was a sick sinking feeling, and it hove to the left. I kept the throttle wide and hit the rudder to the left. It picked up again, shoving me back into the seat, crashing through the stumps as though they were human bones.

I pulled back on the wheel. Then there was something moving at the door. I looked, and there was Ernie's face, desperate. I kicked at the door, pulling back as hard as I could on the wheel. We were lifting, but his face was still in the door. I grabbed the revolver out of my pocket and pointed it at him. We were off the water. He had the door open. I fired. He disappeared. The door slammed shut in the wind.

And then it was deadly smooth. The bright landing lights shone on nothing, stretched forever into the sky. I was climbing fast. I leveled off and flew in a great circle, looking for the river. I turned on some heat.

Then I found the river, shining like obsidian in the inky space below. I checked the compass and headed north.

Sometime later I looked on the seat beside me and saw the revolver. I slowed down, turned the heater on wide, forced the door open, and threw it out. It was very cold for a few minutes, but then it warmed up again. The feeling was coming back into my feet.

After a while the east began to grow pink. The river began to stand out, clear and alive. Up ahead I saw Vicksburg. I swung inland toward the rising sun. It wasn't long before I could see the lake where Arnold and I had taken off.

Part IV

Alice sat in bed by the telephone, in her blue satin bedjacket. It wasn't that she couldn't get up, not even that she was too upset. Of course, the doctor had told her to avoid crises, and this was certainly a crisis. It would certainly have been better for her nerves if this thing weren't happening, or if it could just be happening at some other time in her life. But it wasn't that she couldn't get up, because she had gotten up and she had fixed breakfast and eaten it, and she had had two Elavils, the same amount that she would have taken on any other day. She was staying in bed because that was the most comfortable place to be near the phone.

Her hands smoothed the sheets over her legs, then smoothed her bedjacket. They danced momentarily out of control on the sheets, then came to rest folded in her lap. She leaned back and looked up at the ceiling, breathed one long quivering breath, and tried to start again, "Dear God—dear God—" rocking slightly in her satin bed jacket. But there was really no good in that because she had said it all already all night long, and it was something God should have known already without her even having to say it at all. Still—still, it helped somehow for her to say it. There was something about putting it all into the words, all the breath and feeling. She didn't know whether it would help to try again, whether it would be worth the extra effort. Because she was exhausted. She hadn't slept at all since she had come back and realized that Henry was not here. And where was that maid? Why didn't Negroes have telephones? She didn't really care about that, though. She didn't really care about that or anything else, except for one thing.

There was just the one thing now that she cared about. That one thing was probably what was helping her through the crisis on only two Elavils, and that was that now she wasn't confused anymore. Now she knew. Now she had one thing she cared about no matter what else, and that was she wanted Henry back and alive, and she didn't have any confusion about that at all. Because it was perfectly clear-cut: If Henry was alive and came back to her, she wanted to live; if he was not or did not, she wanted to die.

God should know that by now.

1

That night a certain Mr. Williams was looking forward to his weekend. He had a special room at the north end of the top floor of the mansion where he spent a late hour or two many nights a week, just looking forward to the weekend or sometimes remembering the war.

"Men"—he was planning his talk before his Civil Air Patrol wing—"Now, men, we've been together, most of us, for over two years now. I think we've gotten to know each other, most of us. I think we've gotten to know each other pretty well." Nods and scattered "Yes sirs." "Now I don't see why we shouldn't be able to admit to each other that we all know what a crack unit we are, quit being quite so paranoid about it"—he would chuckle here—"and be able to drop some of this formality and call each other by our first names." Then they would realize that he intended to be magnanimous. That would bring the men closer to him.

And if he put everything on a first-name basis, it would bring them all closer to him. Then they would want to hear it.

Maybe they would just be smoking cigarettes and lounging around by the Coke machine after the meeting was over. Then one of the men would ask him, "Sir, didn't you lose your legs in the war?" And he would be able to tell them. If one would ask, then they would all listen. He would tell them like he had tried to tell his wife, and then, later, his sons, but these men would understand; they would understand and they would listen because they themselves were airmen and a crack unit.

The phone rang.

Who in the hell? "Hello. Williams speaking."

"Hello"—the voice quailed distantly in the earpiece—"Mr. Williams, this is Alice Fargus, Henry's wife."

"Oh, yes, ma'am. And how's the family?"

"Well, that's what I called about. You know we've been out of town the last few days."

"No. I didn't know that."

"Yes, I've been down in Tampa visiting Cynthia and her family."

"Yes, ma'am."

"And Henry went off on a fishing trip."

"Yes?"

"With this friend of his from St. Louis—Dr. Weathermore."

"I see."

"Mr. Williams, they're not home yet."

"I see. And when did you expect them?"

"Two days ago—the day I got back. I didn't know what to do except to call you, cause I know you know Henry, and they went in an airplane."

"Good! Do you know where they went?"

"Down off the coast—some islands."

"Chandeleur Islands?"

"Yes, that's it."

"Uh-huh. And do you happen to know anything about Dr. Weathermore's plane?"

"No, sir."

"Where it was registered or anything?"

"All I know is he was from St. Louis."

"First name?"

"Arnold. Dr. Arnold Weathermore. He's a psychiatrist."

"Good! Now you realize, Mrs. Fargus, that this is generally a matter for the sheriff's department, but in consideration of the fact that you don't know exactly which county this Dr. Weathermore's plane disappeared in, and plus the fact that Dr. Fargus is a personal friend of mine, and in view of the other office that I hold in this state, I think that it is a matter that the Civil Air Patrol could well involve itself in."

"Well—well, thank you, sir. I just didn't know anybody else to call."

"Well, you did exactly the right thing. Now you just try to relax. Everything is in good hands."

"Thank you, sir."

"Everything is under control."

"Thank you, sir."

"Good night, Mrs. Fargus."

"Good night, sir."

He hung up the phone. Henry Fargus, huh? Dr. Hank Fargus! Helluva fine B-17 pilot in the war. Mr. Williams had tried more than once to get Hank Fargus to renew his license and join the CAP, but old Hank, for some unknown reason, could not be made to fly an airplane for love or money. He picked up the phone and dialed Glidden, his second in command.

2

"Well I tell ya how ya go bout it with a sheep," said Charlie, the man sculling in the bow, who was obviously the leader.

"Madre Fonque," said the little man with no name who was from Texas but who had lived for a year in Lake Charles, Louisiana, and who thought Cajuns were very cool. He was sitting right behind Charlie wearing a velour turtleneck above his khakis.

The wooden skiff that they were fishing from was loaded to the gunwales with four men, three ice chests full of beer, one for fish, two cane poles for each man, and assorted tangles and heaps of bait buckets and tackle boxes. The Negro woman that they had brought along for later was sitting sleepily in a puddle in the bottom of the boat, eating a packaged poor-boy sandwich and fingering another.

The dawn was just breaking as Charlie parted a stand of flooded willows and tied the boat. "Ain't that a cat's ass!" said one of the men in the back of the boat pointing to the ice encrusted around the willow trees. Charlie ignored him, reaching into the ice chest, popped a beer, and upturned it against the pink horizon. Charlie had been planning this day for over a week, so he hated that it had turned off so cold. "Shut up," he said to the man in the back. "It'll be sixty degrees by noon. Ain't that right, Tex? Anyhow if it ain't, well me and her goan set the lake boilin'.'"

"Yehoo," Tex said with smoking breath.

"Anyhow, like I was tellin ya bout how to do it with a sheep," Charlie said as the four men began baiting up their poles and dropping the hooks in among the willow roots, "first thing you do is find you a mud hole bout waist-deep—no water, just mud. Then you get you a pair of these hip boots like those rich bastards wear out here to go duck huntin' in."

"Ship the boom! Whap the flotsam!" Tex said as he hoisted a flopping crappie into the boat.

"Break out the beer," said one of the men in the back.

"Would you shut up?" Charlie said. "Can't you tell I'm tryin' to talk?"

They shut up.

"Anyhow, you wrestle the sheep into the mud hole, and you put on your hip boots and get in yourself." Charlie could tell that they weren't listening. He used to be considered an authority on matters such as this. That was mainly back when he used to work at the Billups station, and all the guys would come in and sit around at night. But now he didn't know about this new bunch. "Then you cram the sheep's hind legs down in the boots to hold her steady, and then you flop her out and have at."

He looked around for the men's response. The Negress was looking at him bug-eyed. Finally one of the men in back said, "That oughta get it, Charlie."

The hell with them. He concentrated on his pole. One of the men in the back caught a big crappie; then Tex caught another; and the other man in the back caught one. "Cat's ass, if they ain't in here!"

said one of the men in the back, using the same phrase to express pleasure that he had used before to complain. Tex caught a big one, and one of the men in the back caught a big one. The other man opened a beer. Charlie stared at his cork. He didn't have a bite. He upturned his beer, emptied it, and stared at his cork.

One of the men in the back caught a giant crappie.

"Goddam saddle blanket," said Tex. Charlie stared at his cork. Charlie had a half pint of hardstuff in his tackle box, and he knew that the other men didn't have any of that, just beer.

Somebody caught another one in the back. Charlie reached for his tackle box with a loud clatter. "What's a matter, Charlie, ain't you spittin' on ya hook?" He got out his hardstuff and opened it and upturned it, and it roared down his throat. He ignored the men in the back who didn't have any.

His hardstuff was hot as hell. It burned his throat and even his nose. He tried to cough with his mouth closed so it wouldn't make any noise. He was still holding the bottle when he saw it. He was the only one who could see it, because everyone else was back in the willows, but his end of the boat was sticking out in an opening where he could see out the lake, and it wasn't even making any noise. At first it looked like a UFO, but then Charlie saw that it was an airplane.

It disappeared from the part of the lake that Charlie could see. Charlie looked at his bottle of hardstuff. The other men were looking at their corks. Charlie didn't say anything. His mouth was still burning. He looked back out at the opening; there was no UFO. He put the bottle in his tackle box and slowly turned toward his pole.

Tex caught a saddle blanket and swung it into the side of the nigger lady's head; she screamed and rocked the boat. "Ship the boom! Whap the flotsam!" said one of the men in the back who liked pirate movies. Charlie didn't have a nibble. He wasn't even thinking about his pole anymore.

Charlie reached for the rope and untied it from the willow tree, then picked up his pole and began sculling the boat back out toward the lake. "Hey, what the hell?" "Hey, what's goin' on, Charlie? They in here thickern a cat's ass."

One of the men in the back caught his hook on a snag, and it was

160

stopping the boat. "Get that goddam thing loose," Charlie said without turning around. He felt the line break and kept on paddling.

The day was warming rapidly, or at least Charlie was sweating. He paddled the front end of the boat out into the open lake.

"Goddam it, I knew it!" he said, "and the son of a bitch is sinkin'!"

3

Mr. Williams was in the airport restaurant by six thirty A.M. after talking to Alice at midnight. He had already been by the hangar to start the mechanics gassing and checking out White Lightning. When he went in the door, he saw Glidden with dark circles under his eyes leaning over a coffee cup at a corner table. His stomach turned over. His legs were squeaking badly this morning. He made his way to Glidden's table, and Glidden sat up straight, the sleepiness in his face changing easily to boredom. "Good morning, sir," Glidden said.

Glidden would call me sir if he were executing me, Mr. Williams thought.

"Good morning, Glidden." He sat down and Glidden pushed a paper over in front of him.

He looked at it. "So?" looking back up.

"Do you just want me to notify the Wilkinson County Sheriff Department so we can go on back to work?"

"Back to work?" He'd said that too loud. He forced a composure on his countenance that he didn't feel. At least he hoped it looked like composure. "Now, Glidden," he began.

Glidden stared off at the ceiling.

Mr. Williams managed not to respond to that. "Use your head," he said. "Don't you think that if they'd gone down over land we'd have heard something by now?"

Glidden just looked at him, first shaking, then nodding his head. "Very well—sir—today we'll all take off work and search the Gulf."

4

Goddam sleepy now all of a sudden, Henry Fargus thought as he sat in the airplane, which was now, at last, motionless except for the faint tossing of the wavelets in the lake. He was a long way from any shore, and this should have worried him, because he had noticed sometime during the past ten minutes while he had just been sitting there that the right side of the plane was beginning to sink again. He was exhausted beyond belief, and his mind felt very loaded up like when two radio stations are broadcasting on frequencies so close together that they jam each other and you can't hear either one, or something like that. He wasn't sure he'd ever heard that particular thing happen before, but that's the way he imagined it to himself—with lots of static and confusion. A flock of ducks whistled close over the airplane and landed in a wooded cove off near the shore. He knew all about ducks; he remembered all about them from Robert Collins. Ducks were much better than airplanes because they always landed exactly where they wanted to, no matter how many sticks were in the water. He passed out.

The next thing he know was a blinding flash of blue and red. His head was full of pain, and that woke him up. He had fallen out of his seat and clear across the cabin, because the plane had tilted onto its right side so far. This damn thing is sinking, he thought. It was way over on its side, and the right wing was halfway underwater. Helluva note, he thought, to get through everything I've been through and then split my head open like this just sitting in the plane. Be a lot helluv'er if I were to drown out here too.

He wanted to go to sleep very badly. In fact, if there was anything in the whole world he wanted to do, if some strange man were to come up to him right now and tell him that he could do anything he wanted to in the whole world right now, he would tell that guy he just wanted to go to sleep. His head didn't even hurt so bad if he just didn't have to—oh, hell, it was bleeding. It didn't really excite him that his head was bleeding; it just sort of made him sick. He guessed that in a lot of ways he must be a funny doctor. He didn't really mind the sight of blood, especially as long as it was somebody else's, but the sight of his own made him feel sick and hopeless.

He turned slowly and looked down out of the side window. The glass wasn't two feet from the water. The water had a lot of bubbles rising from it. Then, from somewhere down inside, the realization came to him that he needed to get out of that airplane and onto dry land. But he couldn't figure out how he was going to do that, because the nearest dry land was a half mile off and that water was bound to be very cold.

Forget it, he thought. I just don't feel like—ooooohh—I just don't feel like having—having that to contend with right now.

Henry Fargus looked out the window and down at the water. What good is it going to do just to get out of the plane? he thought. He closed his eyes and went to sleep.

5

"If that ain't a cat's ass!" said Tex.

"Damn if it ain't," said one of the men in the back, throwing a beer can over the side. "What you reckon that is, Charlie?"

"It's a goddam airplane," Charlie said. He was paddling very hard because he could see that it was sinking, and besides, somebody else was bound to come along who might claim his discovery.

"Oh," said the man in the back. "I mean, hail, Charlie, I knowed it was a airplane, but I mean—oh, th' hail with it."

"You mens bettah not go nyah dat thang," said the nigger.

"Shut up, nigger," said Charlie.

"You mens bettah not go nyah dat thang!" she hissed.

"Why the hell not?" said Charlie, still paddling.

"Cause I's skyad of it," she said.

"Fuck you," said Tex, glancing up front for Charlie's approval.

The men in the back tittered. Charlie kept paddling. He was getting closer, but the airplane was sinking fast, and Charlie's arms were getting tired out. He stopped paddling for a second and reached into his tackle box for his hardstuff. Tex looked questioningly, then started to reach for a paddle, but Charlie cut him cold with a look. This was his goddam airplane. When Tex sat back, Charlie opened his bottle and let the hardstuff gurgle into his

163

throat. That stuff took the tired out of his arms and every goddam where else to boot. He picked up the paddle and started pulling again.

The airplane was leaning far over on its right side. The right float was completely under water and about half the right wing. The tail was down too, and the waves were splashing up on it. Charlie didn't know for sure whether it would sink all the way, but it sure as hell looked like it was headed there.

"Hey, Charlie, what you reckon happened? He was just flyin' over and it come uncrunk on him," said one of the men in the back, "cause I didn' hear nothin', when it come down?"

Charlie said nothing. He was paddling hard, and the liquor was buzzing in his head.

"Hey, Charlie," Tex said, "I still can't see nobody in there. Can you?"

"Nope," Charlie said. But he didn't want to talk about that, because when he thought about it, it gave him the same kind of creeps he'd had when he first saw it land and was still scared to say anything about it.

"I swa' ta Gawd you mens bettah not go nyah dat thang," said the nigger, "cause dat's de debil come ta get us fo' me lettin' you-alls haul me outcheah lak this."

"Shut up!" Charlie said.

"Ah swa' ta Gawd you alls betta not do that!" she wailed, and then she tried to stand up in the skiff, lifting her arms to the sky and wailing in misery. She got to her knees and then tried to get the rest of the way up by climbing on top of Tex, and Tex was yelling, "You get off me, you goddam nigger!" and the skiff was tilting, first over to the left and then to the right, and two waves broke over the right gunwale, and the nigger was still screaming, and the boat sloshing from one side to the other, when Charlie turned around and clobbered the woman in the face with the flat part of the pad-dle, and she fell with a terrific jarring thud on top of Tex and one of the men in the back and into the bottom of the skiff.

"Goddam nigger," said Tex.

"Goddam right," said the other man she had fallen on.

"If she moves again, throw her overboard," Charlie said, and he started paddling again.

164

He was pulling down hard on the airplane now, but it was sinking faster than ever. The whole right wing was under, and the left wing was sticking way high up in the air. Charlie thought it was fixing to turn clear over, but he wasn't sure. He was paddling harder than he'd paddled in a long time, and the water was sucking and gurgling around the blades. In another minute he was where he could reach the tail section where it was sticking up, and he pulled the boat along the body and up to the front where the windows were.

"Hey, Charlie," said Tex, "there's somebody in there. Out stone-cold and bloody as hell."

"Thank God," Charlie said. He leaned over and looked in the front window. There was a guy in there that looked as if he was taking a nap, except he had blood all over his face.

"What the hell we goan do?" said one of the men in the back.

"What the hell you thank?" Charlie said. "We goan get him out and haul him in."

"Well, we better git with it," Tex said, "Cause this mothah's sinkin' fast."

"Good thankin', Tex," said Charlie.

"Here, I'm the lightest," Tex said. "Lemme get up on top of there and haul him out, Charlie."

Charlie looked at Tex for a long second. He had wanted to do it all by himself, but Tex was right. It was going to be damn risky, and the lighter the better. "Okay, Tex, go ahead," he said.

"Ship the boom! Whap the flotsam!" said the man in the back.

"Tex, you betta watch yo' step," said the one the nigger had fallen on, "that mothah don't look none too stu'dy to me."

Tex climbed out of the boat and stepped lightly onto the body of the airplane. It sank significantly lower.

"Hey, Charlie," said the one the nigger had fallen on. "Where we goan put him when we get him out? All this black pussy we got in here, I b'lieve if we take on another man this goddam skiff's goan sink."

"He's right," Tex said, prying open the cabin door.

"Shit!" said Charlie.

"We could give her the life preservers and throw her in," said the one she had fallen on.

165

"You mean you'd throw all that good black pussy in the water?" said the one who liked pirate movies.

"Lawsamussy!" screamed all that good black pussy.

"Looks like we goan hafta do something," Tex said, edging the man's shoulders up out of the door. "That bastard needs the ride a helluva lot more'n she does anyway."

"Is he live?" Charlie said.

"Hail, yeah, he's live," Tex said. "He woke up for just a second there."

"Throw 'er in," said Charlie.

"She's done passed out," said the one who liked pirate movies.

"Where's the life preservers?" Charlie said.

"I'll get 'em on her," the one she had fallen on said.

"I just can't b'lieve y'all throwin' all that good black pussy away," said the other.

"Well, y'all better hurry up and do something," Tex said, "cause this mothah's fillin' up pretty fast with the door open."

"I'm ready when you are," the one she had fallen on said.

"Heave away," said Charlie.

They hoisted her up and threw her, she coming suddenly alive in the air, over the side, and she hit with a terrific splash that wet both the men in the back with cold spray. "LawsamussydesdamwhitemensdonethrowedmeintawatahanIkain'tswim—" she was screaming; but Charlie said, "Fuck you," and cut her off. She kept screaming, but Charlie turned his attention now to helping Tex get the man in the boat.

"Hurry up," Tex said. "I'm in water up to my knees now."

"Well, give him here," Charlie said, leaning out and taking the limp man under the shoulders. "Are you sure he's alive, Tex?"

"Goddam right he come alive not three minutes ago. I ain't sayin' he feels real good."

"Looks to me like y'all could at least throwed the beer out instead," said the man who liked pirate movies.

"Have you got him good?" Tex said, "cause I'm fixin' to let go."

"I got him," Charlie said. "Getch' ass back in here."

"I'm comin'," Tex said.

"Look at that black bitch splash," the man the nigger fell on said.

166

"Ship the boom! Whap the flotsam!"

"Goddam motherfuck!" said Tex, slithering into the boat. He was soaked clear up to his waist.

6

The Lake Patrol was just pulling up when Charlie came in sight of the landing. Charlie got a little bit scared whenever the Lake Patrol came around, but he had the Lake Patrol where he wanted it this time. He had what the Lake Patrol was looking for. The Lake Patrol man, John, was big and fat. Charlie called him John Law, but not to his face. John got out of his car and sauntered out on the pier. He always sauntered. He always rattled the change in his pockets when you were talking to him, and he sort of shook to the rhythm of his rattling change like he was nodding his whole body, like he already knew everything you had to say to him, and he was nodding because he didn't have to listen. John was a mean cop, and Charlie hated his guts, but Charlie had John where he wanted him now.

John was standing on the pier, looking out across the lake with field glasses. Charlie couldn't tell whether he was looking at the plane or at the boat. "Hey, the mothah sunk," said one of the men in the back. Charlie looked behind him, and there was just a big swirl in the water. John had put down his glasses. "Goddam John," said Charlie. That was all right though; he'd show him. Charlie was nervous as hell. He could see John waiting for them at the end of the pier, rattling the change in his pockets and not even looking at them.

John did turn and look at them when they pulled the boat up alongside the pier, but he didn't even stoop to help them tie it up. "What you boys got there?" he said with that same expression of his.

Charlie looked up at him from about seven feet below. His mouth was dry, and he hoped to God John couldn't see his hands shaking. "Nobody's neck you coulda saved," he managed.

"Don't look to me like you saved much else," John said, gesturing with his elbow toward the blood that was still running into the bottom of the boat.

"Just fuck you, John," Charlie said. "We saved this guy's life when if he'd of had to wait for you guys, he'd of been at the bottom of the lake by now. So would you just quit actin' so shitty for once and help us get him outa the boat?"

Tex giggled as Charlie turned toward the man.

"Ho' now, don't you touch that body," John said. "We got a ambulance comin'."

"Hoo—excuse my dust," Charlie said. He was on fire inside, but he managed to turn and scramble up onto the pier without looking too awkward.

"Are you being insolent to a officer?" John asked. Charlie noticed a trace of red in his fat cheeks. Tex swallowed a chuckle as he climbed onto the pier.

"Hail, naw," Charlie said. "I'm just doin' his goddam job!" and with that he was off up the pier, fairly running toward the baitshop.

Then Tex and the two men from the back of the boat were up with him, patting him on the back. "That was great, Charlie." "You shore stood that goddam John down." "Way to go, Charlie."

They went inside the baitshop, and Tex went up to the bar. "Beers all around," he said.

"Who's payin'?" asked the woman.

"John Law!" said the one who liked pirate movies.

"Cat's ass!" said the woman.

"I'm payin'," said Tex, "cause Charlie's a hero."

"Hey, Charlie, you reckon they'll put your picture in the paper?"

"They oughta put John's on a billboard. D'you see how red he got when ole Charlie said he'd been doin' his goddam job?"

Charlie was grinning from ear to ear. He sat down on a barstool and suffered Tex to pour cold beer on his head. He took three or four long pulls from the beer can, and then the ambulance pulled up outside. Then there were more cops, and another Lake Patrol man driving a truck and pulling the big Lake Patrol boat on a trailer.

"What the hail they got that thing for?" Charlie said, "we done got him in."

168

"It's all right," Tex said. "John'll straighten 'em out."

"Goddam right," said one of the men in the back.

Then John came inside the baitshop with a man in plain clothes. John gestured toward Charlie and his friends, then waited at the door while the man approached.

"You're the party that brought the man in?" said the man in plain clothes, taking a notebook out of his pocket.

"That's us," said Tex.

"It sho' as hail wadn' John," said the one who liked pirate movies.

"It was me," said Charlie.

"Hey, wait a minute," said Tex.

"Aw, fuck it," said Charlie. "It was me an' Tex."

"I see," said the man. "Pinkston, special investigator for the FAA." He flashed a badge.

"Who?" Charlie said.

"Sounds good enough to me," said one of the men in the back.

"Just like to get your story of what happened," said the man.

"Great!" Tex said. "How bout a beer?"

"Not while I'm workin'."

"Not while he's workin'! Beer for everybody, but this workin' man," Tex yelled at the woman.

"Watch it," Charlie said to Tex.

Tex buried his lip in the beer.

"All right," said the man. "Now what happened?"

Tex looked at Charlie. Charlie took a swallow of beer, ignoring Tex.

John was standing by the door, away from them, rattling his change.

"Wail," Charlie said, "y'see, I'd been promisin' these here guys a fishin' trip for some time now. . . ."

Then Charlie told the FAA man how he had seen the plane go over when they were in the willow trees. He didn't tell him about the way he felt when he first saw it. He told him about the race he'd had to run to get there before the plane sank. He told him about how Tex had dragged the man out and put him in the boat. Then he told him about paddling back in, racing, trying to get there before the man died. "And ole John," he finished up, "he was just standin' there on the pier, wouldn' even help us tie up the boat."

John was standing there, looking bored.

"Well, I certainly do thank you men," said the FAA man.

"We certainly do thank you too," said Tex. He had pulled his lip out of the beer can when Charlie told how he dragged the man out of the sinking plane.

The FAA man nodded and left, and John walked out with him shaking his head.

"What do you thank?" Tex said to Charlie.

"Shit," said Charlie disdainfully.

"Goddam right," said Tex. "Beer all around," he yelled at the woman.

They were all feeling great.

"We oughta have some pussy to celebrate," said Tex.

"Son of a bitch!" said Charlie. "We throwed it all in the water."

"Damn right," said the one who liked pirate movies. "We made all that good black pussy walk the plank."

"Hey, John," yelled Tex.

"John!"

"Hey, you goddam fuzz."

John stuck his now livid face inside the door. "Whadda you want?" he spat.

"Hey, John, we got a little job for you."

"Just so you won't feel left out of everythang."

"Better late than never. Hey, John?"

"What're you bastards talking about?"

"Out there where the plane sank," Tex said, "they's somebody needs your help."

"Looks a lot like your wife," said the one who liked pirate movies.

"Whadda you mean?" said Tex. "John don't need no wife. Can't you see the way he's always got his hands in his pockets?"

The four looked knowingly at each other.

"Shit!" John spat. He slammed the door. Through the window they could see him walking over to the Lake Patrol boat. "Put it in the water," he said to the Lake Patrol man.

"Why?"

"Them bastards done throwed another nigger in the lake," John said.

Charlie upturned his can of beer. Tex clapped him on the back. Charlie thought it was the best day of his entire life.

7

Mr. Williams was very tired, and besides he detested waiting. He had sat for a while in the waiting room of the University Hospital watching the television, and a couple of people had said, "Isn't that Williams? Isn't that Williams?" and somebody had said, "Yes, I think so," but then somebody else had said, "I wonder what that old crook is doing up here," and that had gotten on his nerves, so he had gone down into the hospital cafeteria. Alice Fargus had come down, and he had bought her some coffee. They had talked for a while about their grandchildren, but she had had to go home. She certainly did appreciate his having come by, and it certainly was a relief, Henry being home safe and all. She didn't even seem to know about the other man. Mr. Williams thought she looked like they had given her something pretty strong.

The fact was that she hadn't even seen Henry. Nobody had, and nobody was supposed to for a day or so. Henry was in bad shape—which was why Mr. Williams had to see him tonight and before anybody else did. Glidden was raising hell about that Wilkerson County crap. Glidden was raising hell about everything. Glidden wanted Mr. Williams' ass, and Mr. Williams was in no mood to sit in a hospital all night long waiting for a two-bit pussy doctor to regain consciousness, after having covered half the north end of the Gulf of Mexico looking for him. But Mr. Williams waited. He drank bad coffee. He bought a paper which he didn't read, but which he held up in front of his face anyway just to shut people up. And he waited.

It was after midnight before the intern (whose tuition Mr. Williams had had waived at the Ole Miss Medical Center) tapped him on the shoulder. Mr. Williams jumped and slammed the newspaper down on the table. "He's up, Mr. Williams," the intern said.

"Oh, thank you," Mr. Williams said. "Sit down, Joe."

Joe sat on the edge of a chair.

"How is he, Joe?" Mr. Williams said.

"Seems in good spirits. I told him you were here."

"What did he say?"

"Wanted to know why."

"And what did you tell him, Joe?"

"I told him I didn't know."

"That's right, Joe," Mr. Williams said. He put a hundred dollar bill in Joe's hand. "And furthermore, Joe, from this minute on you don't even know I was here."

"No siree, Mr. Williams. I don't know a thing."

"Now what room's he in?"

"Two fifteen, Mr. Williams. Take that elevator to the second floor, turn right when you get out, and you can't miss it."

"Thank you, Joe," Mr. Williams said, and he made for the elevator, his legs creaking badly.

The hospital walls were very white, and the nurses swished crisply past him. It made him feel how unshowered, unshaven, and bone-tired he was, listening to his creaking legs. He went up in the elevator and found the room. He stood outside for a second before he knocked. His stomach was turning over.

"Hank," he said, rapping lightly.

"Come in," said Fargus' voice.

Mr. Williams opened the door, and it creaked just like his legs. Henry Fargus was propped up on pillows with the reading light on. He, too, looked tired and needed a shave, and there was a large white plaster above his eye. But he smiled when Mr. Williams stepped up to the bed. "Funny that you should come up here tonight," he said.

"Oh?"

"I was just sitting here thinking about what it would be like not to have any legs anymore."

"Hank!"

"No, I mean it." Fargus had a strange expression on his face. "Because I nearly lost mine. Another thirty minutes in that water, they said, and I'd have lost mine."

172

"Oh, I didn't realize—"

"And now it's 65 degrees out there tonight. Another thirty minutes, and I'd have lost my legs; another day, and I wouldn't have even gotten cold. Another day to have left, and none of it would have probably ever happened."

"None of what, Hank?"

"Aw, nothing," Fargus said, closing his eyes. "They gave me a shot a little while ago. I just sort of keep drifting in and out." He opened them and looked pleasantly at Mr. Williams. "Now, what is it that I can do for you?"

Mr. Williams gestured toward the chair near the head of the bed. "Mind if I sit down?"

"Go ahead."

"Hank, did I ever tell you about how I lost my legs?"

"No, sir, Mr. Williams."

"Don't sir me, Hank."

"All right."

"Well, you know I was a P-51 pilot."

"Yes."

"We were based in France, escorting the B-17's that were bombing hell out of Berlin. You were there—you know what it was like."

"I know, Mr. Williams."

"Anyway there I was, just this young kid out saving the country just like we all were. I loved to fly, and I loved the war, and I thought a Kraut was the first cousin to Satan himself."

"I know."

"Well, one day we were up there, and it seemed like the Krauts were throwing everything they had at us. The flak was so thick you couldn't hardly breathe. Two or three squadrons of Me-109's. I'd already gotten one—my second victory, you know—and I was flying high, so to speak. And then it just happened. I never even knew what hit me. One second I was on top of the world—young, wild, flying the prettiest airplane that ever took off, untouchable, so to speak. And the next second, I was just screwed. My airplane looked like it had already crashed before I ever even got out of it, and then, once I did get out, there I was over Kraut territory with no legs. The thing you wanna just yell is, Why? You know?"

173

"Yeah, but you made it, didn't you?"

"If you can call this making it." He gave his hollow legs a vicious slap.

"I'd say you've done pretty well by yourself."

"Yeah, I've done all right. But, Hank, I've been an old man ever since."

Fargus scratched his whiskers.

"So I guess you're wondering what all that has to do with you," Mr. Williams said.

"I was glad for the company."

"I've enjoyed it too, but there are a couple of things I need to talk with you about. That is, if you feel like it."

"Shoot."

"Hank, what about that other fellow that was with you—Arnold Weathermore?"

"What about him?"

"Well, for one thing, where is he? Because they're getting ready to launch an investigation into this thing. I was just wondering if there was anything you stood to lose as a result of anything that might turn up in that investigation, so to speak."

"I haven't"—shaking his head—"I haven't had a chance to think about it."

"Hank, we've been friends a long time. I've handled every legal problem you've had since we've both been in practice. You're the only other man in the whole world that's ever seen Melinda without her panties. We graduated in the same class at Ole Miss."

"Hoity-toity, God Almighty, who in the hell are we?" Hank grinned.

"Ole Miss, by damn," said Mr. Williams. Then he stopped smiling. "Because I don't really know how to say this without going into a lot of needless explanation, but, Hank, both of us stand to lose something from this investigation. You don't know what these things can turn into the way I do. Hank, the things they can drag up, the things just to hurt a man and humiliate him. It could kill us, Hank."

"Why us?"

"I guess it boils down mainly to that I'm your friend."

"And?"

"Well, you know, your wife called me the other night."

"I don't know anything."

"Well, she did. She told me that you were missing—and she said you and Weathermore had planned to fly to the Chandeleur Islands. So this morning I had the CAP wing called up, and we spent the day searching the Gulf between the coast and the islands. We didn't find anything, and tonight we get back and find out that you're already back here.

"Now my problem is that I have this piss-ant of an underling, Glidden, who wants my job as wing commander. Sort of wants my ass too, so to speak. He's raising all kind of hell because I didn't notify the Coast Guard and the Wilkinson County Sheriff's Department and God knows who all else. Well, of course, the reason I didn't was I thought if there was any trouble you might want me on the scene there first, so we could—well, you know—pull all the right strings, so to speak, and avoid any real trouble." Mr. Williams paused.

"So?"

"So Glidden finds out as soon as he gets in that you're already back and in the hospital, so he goes and calls out the Coast Guard and starts pushing his friend down in Wilkinson County for a complete investigation. Now, Hank, I don't have any doubt that your conduct throughout this entire incident has been beyond reproach, but if that goddam investigation ever gets off the ground, then you and me both may be up shit creek. Do you get the picture, Hank?"

"Of course not—which probably means you're absolutely right."

"Huh?"

"No, I'm serious. Isn't that the way it works out? One second you're on top of the world, and the next you're over Kraut territory with no legs?"

"And?"

"And what do you do? You want to yell, Why?"

"Yes."

"Which fits perfectly, considering that's the one thing you can't ever possibly get an explanation for. I understand it perfectly."

"What's that, Hank?"

"Just this—I mean, how many times at how many different parties have I seen you try to tell that story about your legs. And you

175

just want to do that so everybody'll agree with you that it was a real heroic thing for you to do, and so it'll make some sense. Which all fits in perfectly, seeing as it's the one thing in your life, probably, that never will. And it even fits that you'd be telling it to other people."

"Why?"

"Because it's yourself you want to convince."

"Hank, maybe I should have waited until tomorrow."

"No, wait. I'm glad you came. Because I'm with you. I'll do whatever you say. What's more, I sympathize with you about your legs, and even more about your wanting all the time to tell about them. I can't say I understand it. I may never try to understand anything anymore. I still don't even understand why you're here. I mean, if you'll pardon my saying so, you were the last person in the world on my mind, and here you are telling me you're going to solve problems for both of us that I didn't even know we had—which is, I guess, the way most of our problems are. But that's all right. That fits perfectly, and I'm glad you're here, and I'm glad you finally told me about your legs, and anytime you want to tell me again, that's okay too. But I've just got one question."

"What's that?"

"It doesn't ever make sense, does it?"

"Not that I know of."

"So you just might as well start looking for something else."

"You're damn right."

"But what?"

"Well, why don't we start by taking care of this investigation?"

"Good enough!"

"All right. The first thing I need to know is where is Weathermore."

"Where would you like him to be?"

"Huh?"

"Because where he is now, they'll never find him."

"Are you sure of that?"

"Well."

"Yeah, I see what you mean. Well, actually, that is where I want him. Except I want him in the Gulf. Out at sea—sunk!"

"At your service. How's this: Let's see, the third day we were

176

there, there was a big blow that was trying to tear up the plane, and Arnold went out to try to do something to protect it. He never came back. The next day I went out there and found the pontoon smashed. It took me this long to get it fixed enough to get back."

"That ought to do it."

"I hope so."

"You stick by that, and I'll see the investigation stopped."

"My pleasure."

"Dr. Fargus, thank you—for everything."

"Mr. Williams, the same."

8

Henry Fargus was released from the University Hospital on April first. That morning Alice was in and out of the hospital room, busying herself with the details of getting him home, paying the bill, etc. She said little but paused often to straighten his bathrobe or ask him how he was feeling. Then the old battle-axe of a nurse of which every hospital must have at least one, for whom Henry had a strong and long-standing love and admiration and an equally strong and long-standing dislike, rolled him down in a wheelchair, regarding him suspiciously. Alice was nowhere in sight.

"Well, it looks to me like anybody smart enough to be a doctor ought to have better sense'n ta go swimmin' in 25-degree water," she remarked, roughly turning down the back of his bathrobe collar.

"Everything a man does isn't a matter of sense," Fargus answered.

"Men are babies and ought to be kept in playpens so they can't go out and hurt theirselves," Mrs. Gretch said.

"Do you think that would stop them?"

"No. They'd try to escape. Men just have to be heroes and get their cute little bodies all frozen and cut up."

"Don't you approve of heroes?"

"Hero is just one step short of dead man, Dr. Fargus. I don't know what it was you were doing out there in that place where you froze your legs, and I don't want or need to know. I know all I need to about it, and that's that you were feeling like some kind of a hero, and you nearly got yourself killed, and I don't approve of it."

"How do you know I was feeling like a hero?"

"You were hurting, weren't you?"

"Yes."

"Then you felt like a hero. Whenever men begin to hurt, they start feeling like heroes, and so they go and do more and more things to get themselves hurt so they can feel like heroes some more. After a while they get to thinking that just because they got hurt doing something that ought to be enough to make it worth doing."

"Don't you think anything's worth hurting for, Mrs. Gretch?"

"Nothing a man would think of is." Her voice had the slight trace of a quiver. "I've watched you, Henry Fargus. For two years you shut yourself up in that room and don't eat and don't sleep. Drink yourself to sleep at night. And for what? Because you feel like a hero. You ought to be spanked. That would be suffering that was worth something." She stopped pushing the chair. Henry looked up at her. She was crying.

Henry laughed out loud.

She bent down and kissed him viciously above the eye.

Henry smiled up at her.

She went back behind the chair and resumed pushing in silence.

They went down in the clean, fast, air-smooth silence of the elevator and emerged into the spring sunshine through the emergency entrance. Alice was waiting in the purring Cadillac with his bags already in the back seat. Mrs. Gretch and a colored orderly helped Dr. Fargus into the front seat beside her. Mrs. Gretch kissed him again and told him to keep off the legs so they wouldn't sweat too bad later on. And then they went home. Alice drove in silence through the tangled lanes, among the slow, rolling bluffs, and up to the house, the neat, empty house, as Henry imagined it, with the graveyard out back.

"We'll have to get you in by ourselves," she said as she switched off the motor. "That maid hasn't shown up, and I haven't been able to get in touch with her."

"Oh?"

178

"I do wish those Negroes would keep telephones. It looks like with all their civil rights, they would have the decency to keep telephones."

"Well," Henry said, smiling slightly, "if she's not gonna be any more cooperative than that, then we don't need her anyway, do we?"

"No, I suppose not."

So she helped him out and up the stairs into the house. He could walk, but he wasn't supposed to. The only long-term consequence of his frostbitten legs was that he could expect them to perspire heavily from time to time in the future. Staying off them was supposed to keep that to a minimum. Alice had said more than once that she intended to see him do just that.

The house was just as he had anticipated—spotless, neat, and a bit overwarm. His legs immediately started to perspire. "And where would you like to be, darling?" she said, applying ineffectual pressure to his armpits.

"Wherever you are, my love," he said.

"The sitting room?"

"Perfect." He sighed. He hated using crutches.

They went into the sitting room, and she guided him to the chair most nearly in front of the television set. He sat down heavily. She took his crutches. He looked around him. The room was spotless and empty.

"Now, what can I get you?" She smiled, taking a florid afghan from a closet.

"Not that. How about some coffee."

"Oh? What about some tea, or some nice chicken soup? Do you think you ought to be drinking coffee just yet?"

"Coffee!" he said. "Black, raunchy coffee."

"Well"—she smiled slightly, refolding the afghan—"You're the doctor."

"Right," Henry said, and she left. He looked around the room as though he didn't believe it. On the wall above his head was a knick-knack shelf full of tiny pitchers and china figurines. The curtains were printed with tiny milkmaids and had fringe at the bottom. There were vast spaces of white wall. He sat back and closed his eyes.

"Here you are, dear." She handed him a cup and saucer from a tray. Then she set the tray on the tea table and sat down with her own cup. Henry could see the bottom of his cup. On the saucer was a small praline. He ate it.

"How do you like it?" Alice asked.

"Great," he said, "you got any more?"

"Uh-huh. I knew how you liked them, so I made them especially for you to have with your coffee."

"Well, why don't you bring in the box?"

She looked a little startled but went out.

Henry tasted his coffee—lukewarm water.

She came back and handed him three more pralines on a napkin.

He took them and stared.

She sat down.

He ate them whole as fast as he could, then washed them down with the whole cup of coffee. "Delicious!" he said.

She sipped her tea and said nothing.

"Well, it's been a helluva couple of weeks," he said.

"Yes."

"How was Florida?"

"Very nice."

"How are the kids?"

"Just fine."

He nodded and cleared his throat.

"Are you warm enough, dear?"

"Yes. Definitely."

She smiled and sipped her tea.

"There's a lot to talk to you about it."

She nodded, avoiding his face.

"You know that Arnold's dead."

"No. I didn't know."

"He is."

"That's very sad."

"The whole thing was like something out of a nightmare."

"Then don't let's talk about it, Henry." She set her teacup on the table and looked at him, biting her lower lip. "You're back. It's over. Let's just don't bring it up."

"Well?"

180

She stood up—"I'll be right back"—and walked out quickly. Henry heard her in the bathroom taking an Elavil.

He was perspiring all over now. The breath of the heater vent was like cobwebs playing on his face.

She came back and sat down, smiling slightly. She looked at him and picked up her teacup.

"I think I need to go—uh—to the bathroom," Henry said, struggling to his feet.

"Oh. All right." She put her teacup back down and came hesitantly to help him.

"Then I think I'll go up to my study and read a while."

"All right. And I'll go start lunch."

"Fine," he said.

"Fine," she said.

9

Alice left Henry in his study. He sat down in the soft swivel chair behind his desk and looked around. His study was very neat. Alice had given it a thorough cleaning for him. The curtains were drawn and bright sunlight glared against the wide white walls.

Henry had a slight headache. His mail from the past week or so was in the little doggie mailholder that Freddie had made in the school shop, and which Alice sometimes put in his study. He took his mail out and began sorting it—bills into one pile, advertisements into the trash, and his journal and his *Time* magazines into another. Then he scraped up the bills and put them back into the doggie. He set the two magazines side by side in front of him and looked at the covers. *Time* had a picture of Dustin Hoffman on it. His journal was the same as always.

Resolving to do something worthwhile, he shoved *Time* to the rear of the desk and picked up the journal. He looked at the table of contents. There was nothing even remotely related to the yeast problem. Nothing but a catalogue of all the old pussybuggers that used to fill his days. He forced himself to read an article claiming improved statistics on the incidence of uterine cancer in patients using the intra-uterine disc. By the time he finished, his headache was worse.

He looked around the room again. There was something about the air that made him feel like he had cobwebs on his face. He wheeled the chair around so that he could close the curtains, then rolled over to the cabinet where he kept his whiskey. It wasn't there. Had Alice done that? He rolled himself back to the desk and began pulling out drawers. When he found one especially full, he dumped the contents out onto the top of the desk. He went through all of them, and there was no liquor. He pushed the chair back and hoisted his legs up onto the desk top, kicking enough of the junk onto the floor to make room. Then he remembered that he had drunk almost all of it up with the maid. He had left the bottle down in the kitchen. He guessed she had counted it fair game if it was left out down there and thrown it away. The bitch!

He hoisted his legs back down and stood up. Without his crutches, by God! He stood above the desk, looking at the wreckage he had made. Then he kicked his crutches aside and stomped out.

By the time he got to the foot of the stairs, his legs were drenched. Alice came to the door of the sitting room and looked out at him. He glared at her. Her eyes were wet; she had taken another pill. He said nothing. She opened her mouth, but formed no word. Henry made for the door.

He found the Volkswagen keys and got in. He over-revved it backing out of the driveway, and had to slam on the brakes when he got to the end to stay out of the way of a delivery truck. Then he raged off toward the liquor store in his little car.

When he got back, he took the fifth of Wild Turkey out of the sack and threw the sack on the floor of the garage. He shoved the fifth into his pocket and slammed the car door. Then he shoved his hands in his pants and walked around out into the back yard.

Outside, the sunlight was filled with the south wind. Henry had the urge to pull up his pants' legs and let the wind blow on his perspiring skin. Damn fool she was to keep the house so hot. He walked through the grass. It was beginning to get high. Alice would say that it needed cutting, but Henry didn't want it cut. He wanted it to grow up and cover the house. Alice's garden was grown up in dandelions, and the bees and wasps were all out. He kicked at the grass and felt its cold wet mingle with the hot wet of his ankles. He walked clear across the back yard to the hill at the back of the lot that had the animal graveyard at the top. He stopped at the foot of the hill and got out the bottle. He opened it and turned it up in the sunlight. The sunlight was hot in the amber liquid, and the liquid was hot in his throat. He put the bottle back in his pocket and began climbing the hill.

This far from the house he walked more slowly. It wasn't that it hurt his legs to walk, but there was no use making them sweat any more than was necessary. He took the bathrobe off and slung it over his shoulder with the bottle still in it, then stopped and took off his shoes and rolled up his pants' legs. The cold wet grass engulfed his feet.

When he got to the top, he sat down on the collie's grave, facing the pinewood marker. He took out the bottle and hung the bathrobe on the remnants of a cross marking the grave of a cat which Henry had always considered to be anything but a Christian. Across the pine marker was the still legible name Benbow which he himself had painted there over two years before. He opened the bottle and turned it up again this time in the shade, and this time the liquid had a more somber tone. The feeling which this swallow gave him was likewise more mellow and somber. He addressed the headstone in his mind.

Benbow, he said, what now? Do you like it down there in that cool earth? You and Arnold and Ernie? It certainly feels good from up here. I don't think I'd mind being there. The initiation's the thing! Best that I wait and let them tap me. So, in the meantime, what am I going to do?

He upturned the bottle and took a long drink.

That, he intuited himself to think, depends upon what I want to accomplish. Benbow, what do you consider yourself to have accomplished? Nothing? I expected as much. But then you didn't want to accomplish anything, did you? Now there's the difference. You lucky dog. Because you don't even know you're dead without it. You must make the sweetest of fertilizer.

183

I am certain that I would scorch the earth.

Another drink. It was a beautiful day. The grass was delicious between his toes.

Now, Benbow, he thought, we have established *that* I wanted to accomplish. Let us now consider *what* I wanted to accomplish. I shall entertain suggestions from all present. Ah! the heathen pussy-cat suggests that I wanted to accomplish the well-being of pussies. And I say damn all pussies, including you. In the grave, a pussy is a shallow accomplishment.

Benbow? Yes. What then of the Fargus technique? A good question, Benbow. And I can say, that I do intend to complete my work on the Fargus technique. That much I owe to Arnold and Ernie and Robert Collins too, the son of a bitch. And then I think I'll publish it pseudonymously under Robert Collins' name. Along with it, I shall leave to him the responsibility of pondering all questions regarding the value and significance of its accomplishment.

Another drink.

And then I am through with it, Benbow. I have met Robert Collins. I shall finish the Fargus technique. And then I think I'll go to Florida and try to get to know my grandchildren.

Now, if you'll pardon me, I think I'll get drunk. For some reason I keep seeing Ernie's face in the door of that airplane whenever I blink my eyes.